A Kind of Hush

A Kind of Hush

Richard A. Johnson

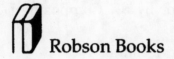

Robson Books

A member of the Chrysalis Group plc

First published in Great Britain in 1999 by
Robson Books, 10 Blenheim Court, Brewery
Road, London N7 9NT

Copyright © 1999 Richard A. Johnson
The right of Richard A. Johnson to be identified as author of this work has been asserted
by him in accordance with the Copyright,
Designs and Patents Act 1988

**British Library Cataloguing in Publication
Data**
A catalogue record for this title is available
from the British Library

ISBN 1 86105 249 9

Typeset in Melior by SX Composing DTP,
Rayleigh, Essex
Printed by Butler & Tanner

Introduction

I was at a party enjoying a quiet drink in a corner, when a person I'd never met before approached and with extended hand congratulated me on writing a book. 'Fabulous!' he said, 'I've always wanted to meet an author.'

I shook his hand and thanked him. He then asked the question that everyone asks – what is it about? I answered that it was about child abuse, and watched for his reaction. His smile faded, to be replaced with a look of concern. He took a sharp intake of breath, hesitated a little, then asked why on earth I would write about such a distressing subject. It was obvious to me that he was feeling just a little uncomfortable. 'Anger,' I said.

'Sorry,' he responded. 'Did you say anger?'

'I did,' I said. 'I wrote it because I was very, very angry.'

Anger is a wonderful motivator. It makes a person do things that they otherwise would never even contemplate. In my case, that anger was mixed with a liberal amount of frustration, and I guess, a certain amount of fear. That combination of emotions enabled me to do what I'd always wanted to do but in a way that I would never have imagined before. It had given me a way of making a point – well, a number of points actually, and by writing it down I could at last get those points over.

But first, I must explain where that anger originated. I come from a very large family. We lived and grew up in the Islington area of London and like most large families never had much to call our own, but not for want of trying by my mother. She would work all of the hours that God sent, just to keep food on our table and clothes on our backs. But we had another disadvantage. I had a father who was a constant sex abuser, not only of his own family, but also others. Added to this he rarely worked and was often drunk. I'm sure that anyone could see that it wasn't the best start in life for his surviving twelve children.

My life, after my father was eventually, and thankfully, taken away from us, was from then on, what one would expect, given the start that I'd had. School, nothing special there, though I do recall writing a story about a young boy who lived at the time the Romans invaded Britain, and being accused of plagiarism by my teacher. I eventually convinced him that the story really had come from my head and not from another writer, but he never apologised. In fact he got my story published in the school magazine and then terrified me by telling me that I would have to read it out at the school concert that Christmas. Not a chance! I was very conveniently sick on that day.

After school it was work. Earn money. Not that easy. I had been entered into the slave labour of an apprenticeship by my mother. To her credit she wanted me to learn a trade, but the money was awful, less than two pounds ten shillings a week. At school I could hang around with my friends, get into trouble, but make a few bob at the same time. That was all gone. I had to be responsible and make an honest living.

Work was not to be the nirvana that most school leavers envisage. It was tiring, dirty, and in my case, very boring. I wanted more, but I never knew what. I changed jobs again and again, and interspersed with some periods of 'ducking and diving', somehow managed to steer a path through life, without actually achieving anything, until I met Barbara.

We've been together over thirty years now and though I've not been perfect, we have brought up three daughters, and have a crop of wonderful grandchildren. Achievement at last. But it was around twenty or so years ago that my life really changed. I became involved again in the world of child sexual abuse.

A girl who was close to us asked for our help. She said that she was being sexually abused by her father. We didn't hesitate. We moved her in with us and started to try to sort out her life. I never realised just how difficult that would be. Nothing had changed. When I was a kid, the social worker that we had was ours by virtue of the fact that she couldn't run as fast as everyone else when our case landed on the desk. That attitude still prevailed. No one wanted to know. I firmly believe that it was because of the ambivalence and almost stubborn intransigence that we met when seeking help for this child that she lost her case against her father. During that time the anger I mentioned previously started to fester.

I became involved in and committed to working with the problem. With the help of a tiny group of people who called themselves the Incest Crisis Line my life took a whole new direction.

Over the following years my home became the head office for the charity and my wife and I opened it up to all kinds of people. We worked at the sharp end of the problem, receiving calls from people involved directly in abusive situations, listening to them, advising them, assisting them to find solutions. It was very hectic and very revealing.

I was astounded to discover that nothing had really changed since I was a child. Many of the agencies involved in the protection of children were indeed just that, protective. Protective of their own part in the process. Those agencies either could not, or would not, work together, and as a result those that they were supposed to be helping often suffered further. Added to this, we were considered to be 'just' a charity, 'just' voluntary workers. We could be ignored, and often were.

The Cleveland case brought much of this seeming failure of cooperation between agencies to the public eye for the first time, with the resulting report highlighting and condemning this fact. It still took a long time before any changes were made.

Our callers were still telling us of bad police attitudes, and poor social services, where sexual abuse was not treated with the seriousness that it deserved. So we, with the help of some sensitive but effective media coverage, embarked on a programme of education.

Now I'm not what anyone at first glance would consider to be a victim. At six feet three and fifteen stones I'm usually left alone if trouble rears its head. But I was raped as a child, and it became obvious to those that I spoke to that if it could happen to me then it could happen to anyone. That message was good, it made people sit up and take notice, it helped those who went through it to accept that they were not alone. The press of course loved it.

As a result of my 'honesty', I was inundated with requests to speak on the subject. Throughout my time with the charity, I appeared on over two hundred radio and television programmes, a worldwide television movie, made by the Norwegian government, chat-shows in the USA and Switzerland, and gave countless lectures and talks for schools, colleges, universities, other help groups, health visitors, probation officers, but far more importantly, various police and social services groups. At last, the message was being received.

When I look back at that involvement, I remember with much pride and affection many of the people that I met during that time: survivors with the courage of lions, to have withstood the hell that they had been forced to live with; police officers, brave enough to defy their seniors and fight for fairer deals for victims; social workers, two of whom lost their jobs rather than accede to the wishes of their superiors; also the many, many voluntary workers out there, who with little or no thought for their own safety protected and comforted those who came forward to help.

But fine words are all very well, it takes a lot more than that to make real and lasting changes. ChildLine came along, and I was and still am very proud to have been a part of its early days. The NSPCC started up a child help line, and as a result powerful voices were added to the fight. Things were slowly changing.

For myself, another new direction beckoned. Worried about the amount of calls we were receiving of current abuse, I took it upon myself to confront the alleged offenders on the behalf of their victims. This could be done in a one-to-one meeting, or by telephone or even mail, and had remarkable results. Abuse would stop! Quite a statement, but on confirmation from those who had asked me for help the abuse did indeed cease. Referrals to therapists were made for those abusers, and often the authorities were involved, but always with the fullest compliance and permission of the one who had first asked for help.

My lectures took on a whole new light. People were fascinated by the new work. No one had realised that victims of abuse often had the best idea of what to do about their situation. No one had realised that confrontation in a non-threatening way often brought situations to an end. I had to explain that many victims, for whatever reason, still loved the person that was abusing them, and would never involve the authorities in their lives. Alternatives had to be devised to deal with this. In Holland at the time was KinderTelephon, a help line for children in abusive situations. It did much the same and was very successful. So it did work.

'But these abusers should be locked up!' I hear you cry. Of course they should, they've broken the law, they are a danger to others. But to whom are we more responsible? If we barge in with police and social services there is a good chance that the victim will not assist, will not give evidence, or even make a statement. Ask anyone who has tried to investigate these crimes. Surely protection of the child must be uppermost in our minds, and if that child has asked for what is happening to be stopped, but not to have its abuser arrested, then why not allow that, at least for the time being. That must be far better than forcing that child to endure its abuse, and to keep the secret for often very many years.

This new work was received well, especially by police and social services. Lecture engagements skyrocketed. I told everyone who wanted to listen what we were about, and was confident that our work would expand and hopefully change the way that we had been dealing with child sexual abuse in the UK. But my confidence was misguided.

I had just finished co-chairing an International Conference on Child Sexual Abuse in central London – a time, I guess, that should have been the peak of anyone's career, when murmurs of dissatisfaction from our counsellors started to reach my ears. I'm still not overly aware of what the problems were, but to be fair other things were occurring that needed my fullest attention. Our treasurer had spirited away most of our funds, something for which she received an eighteen-month prison sentence, and I was arrested on a charge of blackmail. The end of 1989 was a really bad time for me.

I'd stopped a man from sexually abusing his daughter by telling him, at her request, that if he touched her again I would go to the police on her behalf. I then added that it wouldn't be a bad idea if he gave the family the divorce that it deserved, so that they could get on with their lives free from him. I recorded the call so that his family could hear his response.

That it seems is blackmail in the eyes of the law. Well, in that part of the country anyway. I was stunned. Just before New Year's Eve I was arrested and taken all the way to Warminster to be questioned on and charged with blackmail. The funny (if that's the right word) thing is, that my arrest came long after my call to the man; in fact, long after the police had been involved in his home situation, and he'd been tried and convicted of the sexual abuse charges. He was languishing in prison, serving a long sentence when I was arrested. I just couldn't understand what was happening. I'd even, at the time, given the recording of my conversation with the man to his family's solicitor, hardly something that a potential blackmailer would do. It made no difference. The charge was to stand.

During the following eighteen months my life effectively stopped. Stories circulated, allegations and accusations were made, all without foundation, but again it made no difference, the charity fell apart. I couldn't talk to anyone because my case was sub judice, and that made it all worse. The attitude was, if I didn't defend myself publicly then I must be guilty. It was a total no-win situation.

The following year and a half was to be a real eye-opener. Suddenly many of those that I could once proudly call friends, disappeared. I felt betrayed, almost suicidal at times. I had in all innocence put my own security on the line to protect someone from a very profound sex offender, and here I was being treated as a criminal.

In came the frustration. I'd been talking about my methods to police, lawyers, politicians, in fact I'd even discussed those methods in detail on TV and radio on many occasions, and not one person had ever suggested that those methods could have been construed as being illegal in any way. It's no wonder then that I was feeling very frustrated and angry.

Magistrate courts followed. Month after month preparing a defence for things that I hadn't done, things that I still could not understand. I could see no end to it. I took no more calls, my telephone line had been cut off, I received no more mail, my post office box had been diverted. My home was raided by police, and all of my work and files were removed. I was told that they were looking for a wall safe; I don't actually have one but it did give my solicitor and me an insight into the kind of information that these policemen would act on. Someone somewhere was giving them information that was just ridiculous. If it wasn't so destructive it would almost be farcical. I never did find out what they were supposed to be looking for.

It was a week or so from the case, I was to be tried in Bristol. My lawyers had told me not to worry; those that knew the case told me that it could never stand up. My wife and children were equally confident and supportive, but I was the guy in the dock, and when you are in that position, believe me, you worry.

I needed to do something, I was scared, I was frustrated, I was totally disillusioned with our police and prosecution services, but most of all I was angry, very, very, angry.

I started to write. First about me, about my feelings, but I found it far too difficult. I wiped it out, and sat for a long time staring at a blank screen, my years of charity work buzzing through my head. I had thousands of stories, any one of which would defy belief. But all of which I could relate to. I again started to write.

I decided to write the story, as seen through the eyes of a seventeen-year-old boy. This enabled me to detach myself somewhat from my own situation and place it all into the life and experiences of this kid. I chose to use real case histories, but to fictionalise them by changing names, places and so on, and to add to, or lessen some of the incidents written about. The truth is, it is impossible to write a fictional account of incest or child sexual abuse, because anything that one could imagine is, or has been, done to a child in those situations.

Each of the boys is a part of me. The innocence and bewilderment of Si, the obsessiveness of Tony, the bravado of Wivva, the caring of Mick, the internal anger of Alan, the fun loving of the twins, and the nightmares of Stu. I could dump many of my own frustrations on to these characters and in having them deal with it I, in turn, felt better.

I could also rail against the lack of support for these boys, as indeed in my own life there had been a significant lack. The authorities came off pretty badly too, but again only because of experience. I have worked with kids who have been returned time and time again to the very people that are abusing them. I have worked with kids who trust no one but each other, and they need that. They need to be able to connect with someone, and if that someone is another in the same situation, then so be it, at least that someone understands. I have worked with kids almost struck dumb by their experiences and those who try everything, including crime, in an attempt to eradicate the feeling of being victimised. I've seen the effects that people like Stu's father and Gus have on these kids, the almost blind obedience and fear that has been instilled in them, and I've heard many, many times those same kids fantasising about what they would like to do to their abusers.

I've seen families ripped apart by abuse, hundreds of pregnancies every year are the result of unwanted attention upon a daughter by her father. Alison and Jen are real enough, just everyday stories on a helpline. The problem is that many of these kids, after disclosure, are placed in care. Their families often ostracise them for speaking out, and while in care many are exposed to further abuse. It's no wonder that many of them end up on the streets.

I also needed to include something positive, something that none of these boys had. A father figure, someone who would care, someone who would tell them off if needed, someone who wouldn't judge. I needed that when I was a kid, and if I'm honest I needed someone like that before my trial. In came Chef, the father I always wanted. He was to show Stu another side of life, a caring, sharing side. It was intended to confuse the boy, it was intended to make him feel suspicious. Because that is exactly what these boys feel when they meet someone like Chef. No one is that good in their eyes, and it takes a very long time before they can learn to trust and accept true care. I considered having Chef fight for the rights of the boys, but decided against it because at the end of the day they have to help themselves. Recovery is often greatly enhanced by self-help.

The original ending was a happy one – it didn't seem right. In reality, there are very few really happy endings, and my trial was still looming, so I didn't feel that happy.

I left it. I put the story to one side and decided to concentrate all my efforts on my trial.

The day arrived. I'll not bore you with the day-to-day details, just suffice to say that it lasted for eight days, and I won resoundingly, a complete acquittal. So complete in fact that the jury it seems had made up its mind halfway through. This is confirmed by the statement read out to the court on behalf of the jury on the fourth day. It read, and I have to paraphrase here: 'In the unlikely event that we do find Mr Johnson guilty, would you please only fine him the sum of twenty pence.' I was truly stunned and deeply moved by them. My defence continued, and if I had felt up until then that I was alone the following days proved the exact opposite. People were queuing up to testify on my behalf. Policemen, lawyers, charity bosses and workers, an author, a TV presenter, and loads and loads of people that I had worked with or on behalf of. There were also sworn statements from colleagues and friends from America as well as the UK. I knew nothing of all of this, my solicitor thinking it best to wait until the day. I won.

You know it's strange. All through the trial, and the lead up to the trial, I was on the front page of many of the tabloids. Now that I was acquitted, and obviously innocent, I was lucky if I got a mention buried inside the paper. No scandal you see, not newsworthy. It would have been nice if they had just given me one big splash, pronouncing my acquittal. After all I'd sold a few papers for them over the previous weeks. Maybe a splash could have saved the charity. But then again, that doesn't sell papers does it?

Anyway, I could get on with my life. Not so easy. The

charity had gone, and I couldn't get it back. And I have to admit that with all of the hassle and threats that I, and my family, had experienced during that time I couldn't really be sure whether I wanted it back or not. I had learned, in the most complete way, that working with child abuse, and exposing abusers, is a very dangerous occupation. And if the intention was to close down a charity that brought many paedophiles and child abusers to justice then it succeeded. A lot of child abusers could rest happy. More to the point the man who had been allowed to bring the action against me had really won. True, he was in prison, but he got his revenge, courtesy of our legal system.

My euphoria at being acquitted soon abated, reality re-entered my life. I was like a Grand Prix driver, my car chained to the start, wheels spinning like mad, but unaware of which direction to take, and unable to take one anyway. I went back to my book. I gave it a title – 'Getting Even' – this somehow summed up my feelings. I rewrote the ending, leaving it purposefully ambiguous.

I guess Mick sums up how I was feeling, with his stumbling around, trying to find a direction.

Shortly after the trial I was invited to an International Conference in Switzerland, where I was presented with the 1991 Award for Outstanding Service. That was great. I came home with renewed vigour.

I attended a few gatherings here but soon realised that it was not for me any more. I kept meeting people at those places that I'd known for years but who'd kept a very low profile when I needed help. Now they acted as if nothing had happened, some even said that they always knew that I would win. I couldn't take their hypocrisy, it was a world that I no longer wanted to be a part of, a world full of pretentiousness and . . . well . . . not very nice people.

I'd given a copy of my manuscript, as a gift, to a dear American friend while in Switzerland. She called me and told me that someone else in America had heard that I'd been writing, and had asked for a copy. She added that this woman said 'that she knew someone in the business' and that they might help me with it. I'd never thought of doing anything with the work, after all it was just written as an exercise to get rid of the feelings that I was having before the trial. But I relented and said that she could send it if she wanted.

A month or so later I received an envelope from Hollywood. Boy didn't she know someone in the business. My work was being compared to *The Outsiders* and *Boyz 'n the Hood*, both brilliant movies. Of course I was thrilled. But a movie! That couldn't have been further from my mind. Well, it just doesn't happen to working-class blokes does it?

What do I do? I needed an agent. I called some people that I had worked with when doing my TV stuff and dropped in unannounced at the British Film Commission to see if they could help me. They were wonderful. The combination of the two led me to an agent, and she led me to a British film-maker, and the rest is history. There is now a movie called *A Kind of Hush* produced and shot in London, and based on this story. I couldn't be more proud. I was a bit miffed though at the name change. Well, *A Kind of Hush*, what kind of title is that? 'Getting Even' is what I liked because it is what I felt I was doing; but then again things grow on you don't they? And I have to admit that I love the song.

You know I may not be able to work in the way that I used to with child abuse, but in a funny kind of way I may well have found a better way to help. Because, if what I have written helps just one person out there then all of my troubles have been worthwhile.

Richard A Johnson

Chapter One

'Jesus Christ, you'll fucking kill him!' screamed Tony.

'Fuck him,' growled Mick as he pushed the guy's arm across the kerbstone and jumped on it. The crack was sickening. The bloke screamed in obvious agony and tried to lift his arm. It looked as if he had two elbows, one in the normal place and one near his wrist.

'Please, please don't hurt me any more!' wailed the man as Mick quickly rifled through his pockets, stuffed the loot into his jacket, gave the bloke a last swift kick to the side of the head with his steel-tipped DMs and we all legged it.

An hour later we were all sitting in the burger bar. There were eight of us. Mick, nineteen, he sort of looked after us all. Tony, half Italian, seventeen years old, the new boy. Pete and Den, seventeen-year-old twin brothers. Karl 'Wivva K', which is why we called him Wivva, a seventeen-year-old skinhead. Weedy Si whose full name was Simon Gay, poor bastard. His name alone gave the poor sod one hell of a complex. He was just sixteen, on the run from a kids' home in Sussex and in his socks was just four feet, eleven inches of pure dandelion flower with a really aggravating sniffing habit. Then there was

Alan. No one argued with Alan. He was big, built like a tank and had more tattoos on him for an eighteen-year-old than most fifty-year-olds. His only problem was that he was labelled as thick, ESN they called it, but having said that you couldn't wish for a better bloke with you in a rumble. He was unstoppable and never seemed to feel any pain. I once watched five Old Bill try to hold him down and he still got away.

Finally there's me. My name's Stewart, though I prefer to be called Stu. I was seventeen last birthday and I've been with Mick and the gang for about four years now, ever since him, me, Pete and Den had shared a squat in Lewisham.

The burger bar was run by a bloke named Max which is why, I suppose, it was called Max's. It was your typical greasy spoon, and because of where it was, just up the road from King's Cross Station, and the fact that it always seemed to be open, you could always find the place full of kids using the fruit and video machines. It was a hang out for toms, rent boys, drunks, local villains and dealers. And needless to say it was a regular stop on the Old Bill's visiting list.

Max never bothered us, but then Max never bothered anyone. He was the deafest man on earth when he wanted to be and his mouth, like his pocket, was always shut tighter than a duck's arse. You could rely on Max, he never gave credit and he kept a meat cleaver on one side for those who tried to take it. He never listened to anyone's conversations and he never gave advice; we all knew where we stood with Max and we all appreciated him for that.

The only thing that bugged me about him was his

accent, I could never place it, and he always smiled sweetly and winked knowingly but said nothing if anyone asked him where he came from. A story went around once that he was an ex-Gestapo man in hiding. But that would have made him nearly seventy and he didn't look that old, but then again those blokes were supposed to be ultra-healthy weren't they? Anyway, Wivva was convinced that the story was true and thought that he was the greatest thing since sliced bread.

We always met at Max's when we worked King's Cross. We would leave there, do the job, and return there to share out the spoils and plan the next one.

Mick emptied his jacket on to the table.

'Shhhiiit! This bloke was loaded,' hissed Den, as he pulled a gold Amex card from a wallet. Also in the wallet was a wadge of fifties, a couple of twenties and a ten, one Visa card, a couple of small credit cards for a garage and store of some kind, some names and addresses on what looked like torn-out pages from a diary, and an identity card with the bloke's picture on it. Also on the table were two gold chains torn from his neck and an expensive-looking watch with a damaged strap, obviously done when it was snatched from the guy's arm.

I picked up the ID card and saw that the man worked for some big computer company, then I flipped it back on the table. We never really cared who they were, just what they were.

It was late, so we decided to call it a day. Mick split the cash, we got just over forty quid each from this one, that added to what we had made from two earlier jobs gave us about seventy quid each to go home with. Not bad for one night's work. Si took the cards, chains and watch, he had

an uncle who always gave him a good deal on stuff like
that, that's why we let him hang around with us and off
we went on our merry way home, dumping the rest of the
stuff down the nearest drain.

I hate it when I'm alone again after a busy night. I lie in
my bed trying to sleep and all my brain can do is
remember. I've never liked my own company. When I'm
with my friends there's always plenty of action to keep
me busy. I don't have to think, everything is automatic.
But when I'm alone, back come all of the old fears and
memories. I saw a shrink for it once, it did no good.

Chapter Two

When I first met Mick I was thirteen years old, I was on the run from home and I met him in Leicester Square. It was the fourth time that I had run away from home within a year and I knew that if I got caught this time my old man would kill me.

My old man was the reason that I kept on running away. For years he had treated me and my two sisters like shit. I learned later that he was what's called a 'classic psychopath'. I had a few better names for him. He'd hurt people and wouldn't even think about it. Everything he did, he did for his own benefit and he didn't give a shit how many people got hurt in the process.

He had made my big sister pregnant when she was sixteen and went with her for the abortion to make sure that she told everyone that a boyfriend had done it. He slept with both of my sisters regularly while I was there.

My mum pissed off when I was six and I've not seen her since, but my old man has been screwing around with both of my sisters and me for as long as I can remember. The last time I swore would be just that, the last time. He made me give him a blow job in front of the girls, then he went to sleep. It was while he was asleep that I crept out of the house and I've not been back since, four years now.

I was picked up by the Old Bill and put into care two years ago; that's when I told them what was happening at home, but they did nothing. Both of my sisters denied it, can't say as I blame them, he'd have fucking killed them if they'd said anything – and of course he denied it, so nothing was done. That's when I met the shrink.

The psychologist said that if I could talk through in detail with him everything that had happened to me, it would take all of my fears away. Stupid sod. Any fool could see that I was far worse when I left his sessions than I was before I started. He made me feel like it was happening over and over again, and just when I really needed to let loose, he called the end of the session and I had to carry all of the shit that he had awoken in me around for another week. And of course when the next week came, I had shoved it all to the back of my mind again, so it was back to square one. He was next to useless for me. I saw him on telly a few weeks ago telling everyone how to work with kids like me, just like we are a special breed or another race or something. He still hasn't sussed that we are all different and that we all need different things. He knew nothing then and he knows nothing now and it doesn't matter how many letters he has after his name, I can't see that ever changing.

I honestly thought that he could help me, but all he did was ask questions, hundreds and hundreds of questions. I began to wonder who was helping who after a while. I sussed eventually that he was trying to make a name for himself as an expert and was writing a book on kids like me. He wasn't helping me, he was helping himself. Mick found out where I was and sprung me. I've been free ever since.

Mick entered my life after I had just survived two nights under Hungerford Bridge. I had no money, no food and was feeling really pissed off. I was just about to pick a half-eaten hamburger off the top of a waste bin in Leicester Square when a voice beside me said, 'If you eat that, you'll end up in hospital with your guts being pumped out. Come on, I'll buy you a cup of tea and a bacon sandwich.'

I turned and looked at the owner of the voice and saw a boy of about sixteen. He was slightly taller than me, wearing shades and had a pair of Walkman earphones wrapped around his neck. He wore jeans, trainers and an eye-blowing multi-coloured T-shirt with 'Aceeed' printed across the front. He said his name was Mick and added, 'Don't worry, son, I ain't after your arse. If you want some breakfast, come on.'

When you're out there on the street, on your own, tired, hungry and scared, you have to learn to make instant decisions, you learn to go on your instincts. In this case I had two choices. One, go with him and possibly get mixed up in something that could hurt me, or possibly not. Or two, walk the other way and almost definitely get mixed up in something that will hurt me in order to survive. Not much of a choice is there. I chose to go with him – after all nothing worse could happen to me than had already could it? and he did promise me breakfast.

I ate two sausages, bacon, egg, chips and beans and four slices of bread and drank a Coke and three cups of tea. That was probably the best meal that I have ever had in my entire life and all Mick did was sit and grin. When I had finished, Mick threw me a couple of Mars bars and a Coke for later and paid the bill with a ten-pound note taken from a roll of notes in his pocket. He then got up and walked out.

I wondered what the bleeding hell was going on. He can't just be that nice to me and then piss off, I thought, that's not right. I sat there dumbfounded for a few seconds then jumped up from my chair and flew out of there to catch him up, but he'd gone, totally disappeared. I looked left, right, up and down, but he was nowhere to be seen. A crazy kind of despair seemed to descend on me, I felt terrible. Just then a hand slammed down on my shoulder and Mick's voice said, 'What's up mate, you look a bit iffy.'

'Iffy,' I said, 'you frightened the fucking life out of me. Where did you go? I couldn't find you.'

'Sorry mate,' he said. 'Needed a slash, I didn't mean to frighten you. Anyway I think we need to talk, I'd like you to meet some friends of mine.' He took me back to his squat.

A big Victorian place it was. The front was boarded up, but we got in by walking up an alley behind the row of houses, jumping a wall, through the garden and in a back window. As we climbed in I could hear loud rock and roll music coming from one of the rooms upstairs.

'Good, they're in,' Mick said as we climbed the stairs.

In a back room on the first floor two boys were sitting on an old settee. They were drinking from cans of beer and singing along with a 'Quo' number on the radio.

Mick shouted: 'Hi guys, I've got a new one for us.' They were like two peas in a pod. Both were in denims and white trainers, both had the same hairstyle, both had the same 'Quo' T-shirt; in fact the only thing that was different about them was a hanky tied around their left arms.

They looked over and grinned.

'What's your name then,' said one and without waiting for an answer went on to say, 'my name's Den and that's Pete', pointing to the other boy.

'No, I'm Den,' said the other boy, 'he's Pete.'

'No, I'm not,' said the first, 'I was Pete last week, it's your turn now,' and pretended to be upset.

The other boy then said, 'You weren't, it was me, I'm getting a bit cheesed off at you always choosing who you want to be.'

'Tell you what then,' said the first. 'We'll both be Den and Pete this week and see how that works,' then they collapsed into fits of laughter.

'Ignore them,' said Mick. 'Being twins they spend most of their time trying to fuck people's minds up.' He then explained that Pete always wore a yellow hanky tied around his arm and Den a red one, at which point both boys promptly removed their armbands and swapped them over, then collapsed again into hysterics.

'You're fucking mental, you two,' said Mick with a grin as he collapsed on to the old settee and threw me a beer. I never was quite sure who was who between them after that.

During that week we did a lot of talking. I dumped a lot of what had happened to me on them and was stunned to find that they too had been through very similar experiences. I was even more shocked when Mick told me that he'd seemed to know what I had been through when he first saw me in Leicester Square, although now I understand. It is true you know, kids like us do recognise each other even though we may not know it at the time.

Mick was sexually abused in care. He was put into care when his mother took to the bottle, he was just seven at the time. He stayed there until he was thirteen, when his sister managed to get him out to live with her and her husband.

During his time in care he was 'looked after' by a man that everyone had to call 'Uncle Jack'. Uncle Jack, it seems, was a residential social worker with some fifteen years' experience of working with disturbed kids. He would take the kids on outings to places like the zoo and Madame Tussaud's and also on holidays to camps and adventure weekends and stuff like that.

Uncle Jack loved his camera and was always taking pictures of the kids, the trouble was that many of the kids didn't like the kind of pictures that Uncle Jack was into. Mick said that it all started quite innocently. He would snap them swimming, climbing and playing games, but then it became more unnerving. He would creep into the showers and snap them, or their dormitories or rooms as they prepared themselves for bed. Some of the kids told him that they didn't like him doing it, so he started to give them presents of money or cigarettes if they would pose for him.

You know, kids who need love and attention will often do anything to get it. Mick admitted that he was one of these and as a result got involved with five or six other kids as regular models for Uncle Jack. These kids, boys and girls between the ages of seven and thirteen (they were moved on to another home when they reached thirteen), were eventually doing everything you could imagine for his camera.

Mick said that one girl, she was twelve, was photographed giving two hand jobs and one blow job to three boys, including Mick, whilst having full sex with Uncle Jack, all at the same time. She got twenty Rothmans and £1.20p for that.

Uncle Jack got caught when he tried to bugger one of the new boys. The kid screamed the place down and it frightened the life out of the old bastard. An investigation began, but it was dumped when he resigned and retired to the coast. Before he left, Mick and three other boys blew up his Morris Countryman by sticking a whole bundle of bangers in the petrol tank on bonfire night. Other than that one incident Mick has no fond memories of his time in care at all. He's now a chain-smoking delivery driver, living alone in the flat that his sister used to have in Hackney.

Pete and Den were abused by a schoolteacher. They were eleven years old, their first year in high school. They took with them their reputation for fucking about and used to drive their first-year teacher absolutely loopy by pretending to be the other one all of the time. One day he had taken just enough from them so he sent them to the headmaster. The Head wasn't in but the Deputy Head was. He caned them both, trousers down, bare arsed and instructed them to stay after school every night for a week. By the end of that week he had buggered the pair of them and made them bugger each other. That was so they didn't tell everyone.

You see if you're involved, you're responsible, and if

you're responsible you don't tell. Clever bastards nonces, if they don't get you one way they'll get you another.

Mick was in the fourth year at their school when he sussed out what was happening to them. He and five friends 'convinced' the Deputy Head to leave. The twins never told anyone but us, they couldn't you see, they felt that they were guilty too. Mick never told them how he had convinced the old guy to leave.

My first week at the squat was spent resting and relaxing. It was great to feel warm and comfortable. No hassle, no pressure, no fears. Mick was out till quite late most nights and Pete and Den, or is it Den and Pete, took me around with them.

I needed some clothes and other bits and pieces so they decided to take me shopping; well that's what I thought they were going to do, but boy was I in for an education.

First they would take me into one of the best clothing stores in the local shopping centre and let me choose whatever I wanted. I wasn't to actually pick it up, just show it to them. I was having a great time picking out some very expensive stuff, pretending that I could afford it and thinking to myself that this was a fun way of killing some time, when they gave me some money and told me to go and sit in the cafeteria overlooking the shop. Situated on a sort of balcony, from my table by the rail I could drink my coffee and watch everything that was going on.

I watched as Pete took a stack of clothes to the shop assistant who gave him a ticket for the changing-rooms, Den was over by the far side of the shop out of sight at this time. He waited until the assistant's attention was distracted by someone or something else, which wasn't long in a place of that size, and quickly moved in hugging a pile of clothes that he had picked up. As he passed the changing-room door, Pete slipped him his ticket and with Pete's ticket and the pile of clothes that he had, he came up on the assistant from behind and gave the whole lot to her, saying that he didn't like them. She, thinking that Den was Pete, took them with the usual shop assistant's scowl and began sorting them out for returning to the racks. Den would then keep her attention by talking to her whilst Pete would slip out behind her with the pile that he had for me.

As they were only allowed to take three items at a time into the changing-rooms, it took seven different stores before we decided to call a halt. By the end of that day I was the one who was getting the assistant's attention while Pete and Den did their swapover. It was the sweetest thing that I had ever seen, electronic tags were found dumped in changing-rooms all over the place.

I also discovered how the boys had so much money. What I heard frightened yet excited me. Mick called it 'getting even'. Pete and Den said that it made them feel magic when they did it. They felt that they could at last feel control over something in their lives.

What they were doing was setting up and rolling nonces, dirty old men, just like mine.

One of the boys would stand as bait, wait until he was approached by one of these guys and walk off with him to a quiet spot to do business. Unfortunately for the bloke, half-a-dozen other boys would be waiting and the only business that he would get would be the loss of any cash or valuables that he was carrying, a good kicking and a visit to a local hospital. It was sweet, they never complained (well, they wouldn't would they), and with any luck another nonce might just think twice before ever touching a kid again.

It sounded brilliant. My mind turned to thoughts of setting up my old man like that and I asked Mick about it.

'Later,' said Mick. 'I want you to meet some of the others first.'

Chapter Three

That night Mick drove us across to King's Cross in a pure white Golf GTi. This motor had everything – soft top, radio, stereo cassette blasting out Acid House music, even a phone.

I asked where he had got it from and he replied, 'Ask no questions and I'll tell you no lies,' then he winked.

Den chipped in with, 'You've got to learn Stewy boy, when you want something in this world you can't sit back and wait for it, you've got to go out and get it.' Just then the car phone rang, we all jumped.

Mick picked it up. 'Hello,' he said softly. He listened for a second or two then yelled.

'Fucking hell, it's the geezer who owns this motor!'

Pete and Den creased up with laughter. I could hear the poor bastard screaming down the phone to Mick.

'I'll get you, you bastards, you see if I don't!'

Mick laughed, said goodbye very sweetly and hung up on him.

'If he'd been nice,' he said, 'I'd have told him where I was going to leave it. But no, the silly bugger had to threaten me, didn't he? Well now he's gonna have to look for it.' I thought that Pete was going to bust something, the way he was laughing.

Mick parked the car up in an old garage behind some flats off York Way.

'Find that, you bastard,' he said as he walked away taking with him the bloke's cassettes and mobile phone. 'Might as well use it till the batteries run out,' he said, stuffing the phone into his jacket.

We arrived for my first visit to Max's and joined five boys who were sitting at a corner table. Mick introduced me to them. There was Alan, not so big then. Wivva complaining that the barber had sliced open a couple of zits when he gave him his skinhead cut earlier that day. Trev, who was off to join the Army next week, and Mark and Steven.

Steven delighted in telling everyone that the Old Bill were on his arse again for kicking his old man in the bollocks.

'I'm not worried though,' he said, 'I'll stay at my gran's for a few days and they'll forget all about me.' Then he said, 'I've got to get some dosh though, I don't want my gran to be out of pocket because of me, poor old girl's only got her pension.'

Wivva's grandad was a war hero, won the George or is it Military Cross or something at Tripoli, lost a leg in the process. Wivva was fascinated with the stories that he used to tell him about those days and ever since has wanted to be in the SAS.

He used to massage his grandad's back and shoulders for him when his war wounds started to act up. That graduated to 'jacking him off' because grandad said that it was good for the pain. Wivva never knew that it was wrong, he never even suspected.

Until his mum caught him wanking himself in his bed one morning. She kicked him all over the house screaming, 'dirty bastard dirty bastard!' at him. He was so confused, poor fucker, that he went straight to his grandad. When he told him, the old bastard had a heart-attack. He died a month later.

Wivva had learned in the worst way possible that he had been abused. And even worse, his grandad had been his abuser. But he couldn't make sense of it. So he took all of his anger out on everyone else, especially nonces. Wivva loved his grandad and for some weird reason still does. We never question that.

He still lived with his mum and dad, but often after he'd finished work (he was an apprentice painter and decorator) he came to spend his nights with us.

Alan was most definitely one of a kind. Built like a brick shithouse no one, but no one got up his nose. I swear he could break your back just by looking at you; he was every inch a tough guy. He worked for a demolition firm, just right for him that was.

Alan never talked about his past but we all knew about him because we had read it in the papers. He was one of a load of boys that had been screwed by the headmaster at a special residential school. He hated nonces so much that it hurt. He lived with his invalid grandma and often said that she drove him fucking mental with her 'Do this love' and 'Do that love'. He put up with it because it was rent free and quite frankly, because no one else in his family wanted him.

Just like me every one of them had been sexually abused and not one of us had got any justice at all. We

were all bloody angry at the way that we had been
treated, angry at a system that didn't seem to care, the
police for doing nothing, the social services for giving us
no choices, our families for letting us down, but most of
all, almost murderously angry at the type of people who
had used us. It's for that last reason that we chose to do
what we did during the long weekend nights.

Mick explained what was going to happen and said
that as I was the new boy, I could sit back and watch.
Mark was the bait for that night. He was fifteen but looked
about twelve and a half. He was the classic choirboy type,
blond hair cut into a pageboy style and big blue eyes. But
as I was soon to learn, looks can be deceptive – that boy
was as hard as nails.

Trev disappeared and reappeared ten minutes later.

'It's looking real cool,' he said. 'I think there's a chance
of some big business tonight.'

'Right,' said Mick, 'let's go.'

Mark went ahead and set himself up at the front of
King's Cross Station, leaning against one of the metal
posts that hold up the canopy. Mick, Alan and me sat on
the floor by the main entrance doors.

'So that we can keep an eye on him,' said Mick.

The others went through a side entrance in York Way
and cut through the station to an exit near the taxi rank
on the other side. They then cut a right and disappeared
into the tiny side-streets behind the station.

We watched Mark for what seemed like ages before
someone approached him. The man talked to him for a
few seconds and then walked off. Mark mouthed something to Mick, chuckled and went back to his business.

'No sweat,' he said. 'He wanted to know if Mark

wanted to buy anything.'

'Like what?' I said.

'Drugs,' said Mick.

'Oh, is there much here then?'

'Too fucking much,' said Mick and added, 'sometimes these blokes can be fucking dangerous, so you've gotta be very careful. Anyway, if you ever need any of that shit let me know, I can get it far cheaper than they can and a lot better quality.'

'I'll go along with that,' said Alan with a grin.

A few short minutes later someone else stopped to talk to Mark. Mark put his hand in his pocket as he spoke to the man.

'This is it,' said Mick. 'We've got one, come on chaps.'

We got up and walked slowly through the station and round to the back where the others were waiting.

Alan explained that the signal for catching a live one was to put your right hand in your trouser pocket when talking to him, that way everyone could see and could get ready for action.

We all crouched down behind a wall and waited.

I heard Mark arrive and through a break in the wall saw him lead the bloke into a doorway. Mick whispered to me to stay put no matter what happens and then got himself ready to move.

The man unzipped his fly exposing his very ready penis, and at that moment Mick screamed Go! and everyone except me jumped over the wall and piled into the doorway. I swear that bloke literally shat himself, I have honestly never seen anyone as scared as that in my entire life. He threw himself into the corner and rolled up into a ball.

'Fucking perv, fucking perv!' shouted Wivva as he kicked out at the guy's head, the others were just kicking and punching anything of him that was showing.

He went quiet. Mick pulled everyone off and went through his pockets, checked his neck for chains and ripped off his watch.

I came out from behind the wall, I was shaking like a leaf. I looked at the bloke on the floor and felt sick.

Mick hissed at me, 'Kick him, he's just like your old man, kick the slag.'

Suddenly all I could see was a picture of my old man in front of my eyes. All of the anger and fear that I had felt when he was around welled up inside me as I looked down at this creep now lying curled up in the corner of the doorway. I kicked him hard between his legs from behind. He moaned. I kicked him again and again, tears from years of pent-up anger and frustration flooding down my face as I screamed obscenities at him. Mick grabbed me from behind, Pete and Den took hold of my arms and we ran.

Up by the old gas holders, along Goods Way to York Way, through Wharfdale Road to the Caledonian Road and back down to Max's.

We were high. Not one of us had taken anything, no drugs, no booze, nothing, yet we were all higher than I had ever thought it possible to be.

'Burger and chips all round lads?' asked Max as we danced in.

'Too right,' chorused Mick, Trev and Mark as we moved to our corner and sat down. We waited until we had finished our food and Cokes before Mick took a look at what we had taken from the guy.

There was a wallet with eighty-five pounds in it, a Visa card, an Access card, a picture of a bloke with an old lady and an identity card that showed that he was fifty-three years old and worked as a manager for a TV rental company.

'Just think,' said Mark, 'we could be renting our telly from that slag.'

Mick was grinning again. 'Look at this then lads,' he said. In a long brown envelope, taken from the bloke's inside pocket, was a whole wadge of notes.

'Must be his shop takings,' said Trev.

'Who cares,' said Steven. 'It solves my fucking problem.' Everyone laughed. Four hundred and sixty-two pounds was in that envelope.

We did one more that night, a short, squat, greasy-looking bloke it was. He tried to drag Mark into his car in the hotel car park, but we stopped him. He got really done, and when Mick checked his pockets and found that the bastard had no money on him at all, he got done all over again. Mark was so mad he bit the bloke's fucking ear off.

Chapter Four

Things remained much the same for about four years. As we got older some of us tried to get our lives into some sort of order, you know, jobs, a decent place to live, that sort of thing. The squat was pulled down so I went and found myself a job as a trainee chef for a Bayswater hotel where I lived in. Trev joined the army and we lost touch. Steve's in prison, he got five years for almost killing his old man. And Mark? Well, believe it or not, Mark's at university. He's studying computers, it seems he was a whiz-kid with them at school.

Weedy Si has been with us for about eight months now and when he's not staying at his uncle's place in Kennington he crashes with one or other of us.

Si's mum and dad were hippies. They were well into all of that free love and drugs stuff. Often Si would be woken up by the grunts and moans of couples screwing each other all over the flat. His parents were into wife swapping, husband swapping, every sort of swapping you can think of. There was so much shit smoked at his gaff that he was addicted to it himself by the time he was ten.

They got themselves involved with some people who

ran a witches' coven or something; it was really just an excuse for more orgies, but they had ceremonies and special days when kids had to be there. It was at one of these, in an old church off Old Street, that his mum and dad, both stoned out of their heads, had sex with him while everyone else there watched. The police raided the place and caught them at it. Both his parents were given probation and Si was taken into care. He's been running away ever since.

The only one in his life, other than us, who he trusts, is his uncle Chris, that's his mum's brother. Chris offered to take him in, but the social services for some reason keep saying no. I suppose that it could be that Chris has a record for violence, ABH, GBH, that sort of stuff. Chris says, quite innocently, that it was only because he was protecting himself; what he doesn't say is that he was protecting himself from being caught at one or other of the blags that he was doing.

When Si can't stay at Chris's he sleeps on the streets 'working' the stations for food money; that was until he met us of course.

Si turned out to be very useful. Mick could never get good deals on the stuff that we took from the nonces; that was until Si took some of it to his uncle Chris, now we can sell on anything. Cash cards, credit cards, driving licences, you name it, Uncle Chris can deal with it, very handy that is. I just wish that dirty sod Si would learn how to use a hanky, his constant sniffing drives me bleeding mad. Oh! the other thing about Si is that he is brilliant as bait and that's mainly because he'd been working on the rent boy scene for some two years before we met him. He knew those punters inside out and could always pick out the best ones.

Tony's the new boy. He's the result of a holiday
romance. You know how it is. Mum and a couple of
girlfriends go off on one of those 18–30 holidays, she gets
swept off her feet by this butch Italian waiter, he swears
his undying love, says that he wants to take her home to
meet his family (after the holiday season is over of
course). He sees her off at the airport and says that he'll
write, and never does. She gets home and a short time
later realises that she's been knocked up. She's blamed
Tony for it ever since, seems the poor bastard looks just
like his dad. She eventually put him into care because,
she said, she 'couldn't cope'.

Tony was fostered by a pervert. It happens a lot.
Dumped by his mother, fostered out to this bloke and his
wife, then forgotten about by his social worker.

Tony could never understand how the council could
let a childless middle-aged couple be foster parents.
Come to think of it, it does seem pretty strange doesn't it?
If a kid's got to learn what it's like to be a part of a caring,
loving family, you would think that they would put him
in with a family that had kids, wouldn't you? Anyway,
the foster father started on Tony almost from the day he
arrived and he couldn't tell his social worker, after all it
was her that had put him there.

He left there at sixteen and has been working as a
London Transport apprentice ever since. He's got a bedsit
over near the Angel and just like Si he met us on one of
his bored-shitless nights when we were hanging around
at Max's.

That night was Tony's first, Wivva brought him in.
Wivva had been seeing a lot of Tony since we first met at

Max's. He had that look in his eyes that I must have had after my first one, and just like me, he wanted to go out again.

Mick had a 'special' laid on for the next night.

Chapter Five

It was six o'clock on a Saturday morning. Big day at work and I was still shattered from the excitement of the night before. Couldn't be late though, if I lost my job I'd be bumming beds on friends' floors again and I didn't fancy that. If I'm quick, I thought, I can grab some juice and coffee in the dining-room before the rush starts.

I jumped out of bed and pulled on a fresh pair of blue and white striped chef's trousers, a nice white T-shirt and jacket and checked that my hat and apron were okay. The apron was dirty and I didn't have a spare. Shit! I thought, Chef would kill me if I turned up without a clean one. No sweat though.

I crept out of my room and along the hall. I stopped and listened at the door three rooms down from mine. 'Good, he's in the shower,' I whispered to myself. I carefully opened the door halfway, just enough for me to see his outline through the shower door. I dropped to my knees and crawled over to a small chest of drawers that was against the wall between me and him and silently opened the bottom drawer. I slipped out an apron, closed the drawer and quickly slipped back out of the room and into the hall; then whistling loudly, I strutted down the hall to the lift and went down to work.

George lived in that room. George was a shit. He came from Hong Kong and he's related in some way to the owner of the hotel. George wants to be the best chef that Hong Kong has ever seen. The trouble is that George is a walking disaster area, added to which he thinks he's brilliant. Chef thinks that he's a right tosspot but can't get rid of him and you have a wonderful combination for a very happy kitchen.

Two orange juices and three coffees later and I'm in Chef's office waiting for his instructions for that day's function.

'Where's George!' hollers Chef.

'Dunno, Chef,' I said, looking as innocent as I could.

'Go and find him, Liz,' he said to one of the kitchen hands and off she trotted.

'Might as well have a smoke while we wait for his lordship,' said Chef as he lit his second cigarette of a sixty-a-day habit.

George came in looking all flustered.

'You're improperly dressed,' barked Chef. 'Where's your apron?'

'My apron,' said George, 'it just vanish.'

'What do you mean, vanish?' asked Chef.

'It there, then it not there,' said George.

'Maybe the roaches took it, George,' I said, trying hard not to grin.

'Knock it on the head, lad,' said Chef, looking at me with a scowl.

'I know it when I see it,' said George, 'my mother, she sew my name in corner.'

'Well, she would wouldn't she?' I whispered to myself.

He insisted on looking at the corner of my apron.

I told him to piss off.

'Come on, boy, show him,' said Chef, 'or we'll never get any work done.' George lifted up my apron and checked the corner. He studied it carefully then looked up at me. I thought that he was going to cry for a minute, his eyes behind his Coke bottle glasses just filled up. I felt myself feeling quite sorry for the snivelling git, but only for a couple of seconds. Chef then gave him a lecture about being properly prepared and said that he could learn a lot if he followed my example. Fucking good job I bit his name off the apron in the lift on my way down.

Chef's okay. I don't know what his real name is, everybody calls him Chef, even his wife. He likes to tell everyone stories about the time that he studied and learned his profession at Escoffier's in France. Lying sod. We all knew that he came from the Royal Army Catering Corps. But he was good, very good.

He was a big bloke, nineteen or twenty stone with a bright red face mostly covered by his full set of beard and moustache that was a dingy grey colour with tobacco stains tinting it here and there. He had sparkling blue eyes half-hidden behind a pair of half-moon specs, and massive hands. He just oozed niceness if you know what I mean.

I used to talk lots to Chef. He became for me just what I wanted my dad to be. He always used to come out with things like:

'How can anyone with such obvious intelligence spend so much of their life trying to hurt everyone else.' That was aimed at some of the tabloid reporters. And:

'While you are a part of the problem, you can never be a part of the solution.' That pearl of wisdom was aimed at the shrink that I had told him about. He was great and I'm not ashamed to admit that I loved that man.

Anyway, the day was to be taken up with providing the food for a function for one hundred and fifty people. By eleven o'clock most of the main cooking and preparation had either been done or was well on the way, when Chef called me into his office.

'Sit down, son,' he said.

'What's up, Chef?' I asked.

'I'm going to ask you to do a very important job for me,' he said. 'As you know we are going to be running a carvery for these people at lunchtime and I want you to do the carving.'

Now let me explain. There is only one thing that Chef likes more than cooking a successful meal, and that is being told that he has cooked a successful meal. For that reason Chef always carved and served the meat at any major functions. He just loved the look of pleasure on people's faces as they bit into his cooking. So you must understand that this was not only more than strange, but for me was one of the highest honours that he could give me.

I asked him why and he said, 'Just do the job, son, and don't let me down.'

George didn't like it. George thought that he should be doing it and George said so. Silly thing to do that was. You don't show off in a kitchen when everyone in that kitchen thinks you are a shit. We all decided to teach George a lesson, even Chef.

George was called into Chef's office and told to prepare

a large bowl of chocolate mousse for the function. We all knew that George loved his belly and his belly loved chocolate mousse. He came out of the office grinning from ear to ear.

'Chef want me to make my special chocolate mousse,' he crowed.

We watched as he gathered all of the ingredients together and began his preparation. Chef sent Liz to the chemist in the hotel foyer with a note. She returned ten minutes later with something in a paper bag.

George was merrily whipping up a batch of egg whites while waiting for some slabs of plain chocolate and butter to melt in another pan. He whipped some egg yolks and water into the chocolate mixture and then started to fold in the egg whites.

Now George is one of those people that, if you ask him to prepare something, only seventy per cent of it would reach the table, he will have eaten the rest during preparation. His mouth was already full of chocolate.

When he had finished the mixture, he went to get a large cut-glass serving dish to pour it into. While he was gone Chef emptied the contents of the paper bag into the mousse and gently folded it in.

George came back and poured the mixture into the serving bowl, making sure that he left plenty behind for himself, then he put the serving bowl into the fridge. The rest, well over a pint, he wolfed down without taking a breath.

A while later, Chef yelled, 'Where's George?'

'In the bog!' I yelled back.

'Again!' Chef shouted and walked off roaring with laughter.

Almost half a pound of Senokot Crystals went into that mousse – George must have shit his brains out that day.

Nice clean whites, courtesy of the laundry-room. Clean and newly sharpened knives at the ready, I stood at the carvery and prepared myself for the incoming lunch guests. George was still shitting.

They filed into the dining-room in perfect order, too perfect if you ask me. Then I understood why Chef had decided to stay in the kitchen this time. It was the bloody army, we were catering for an army reunion function and judging by the letters on one or two of the uniforms, some of them were from the Royal Army Catering Corps. The crafty bastard. He wasn't giving me any honours at all, he was trying to avoid meeting any of his old mates.

I turned and looked towards the kitchen and there, behind the steam-coated round window in the kitchen door, was Chef grinning from ear to ear. It was good to know that not even he was perfect. Behind him, George, holding his arse, was rushing back to the bog again.

Chapter Six

'What do pervs have after dinner!' yelled Wivva.

'Piss off Wivva!' we all shouted back.

'You've heard it,' he said with a moan.

'Course we have,' said Pete, 'we've heard all your bloody jokes.'

'We told most of them to you in the first place,' said Den.

'One day,' said Wivva, 'one day I'm gonna find a joke that none of you have heard.' We all laughed at him.

We were all sitting in Max's preparing for the special and waiting for Mick.

A 'special' is when we all go for someone who has hurt one of us in the past. This one is for Tony. Wivva told Mick that Tony's foster father is going to be at some pub in Willesden for a stag night and we are going to get him when he comes out.

Mick arrived in his van. He's allowed to use it at night because he has early morning starts for his delivery job. We all go out and pile into it and as we drive to Willesden, Wivva explains the plan.

It seems that this guy would have to walk from the pub, down the length of Willesden Lane to Kilburn High Road, then he has to take a night bus home. We are going to be parked up on Willesden Lane and we are going to wait until he comes along and drag him into the back of the van. He's not going to know what is happening because he'll be far too pissed.

We drive off. We parked up by Coverdale Road and waited.

Everybody goes deadly quiet just before a special. The only sounds come from the cassette. The music is Tony's, it's his special so he chooses the sounds. True to his roots, he's into ballads, Italian American, Frank Sinatra, Tony Bennett, Perry Como, that sort of stuff.

Specials are different, this is someone that is known to us. We can make sure that this one knows just why he's getting done. We all sit and wait. Eight heads with eight different thoughts.

Me, I was thinking about when the time would come for me to get my old man and what I'd do to the bastard.

Mick was sitting and talking quietly to Tony. I know what he was saying, I've seen it and heard it all before. Old head on young shoulders is Mick. Tony Bennett was softly crooning 'If I Ruled the World' while we waited.

It'd been pissing down with rain for some ten minutes, Alan said that he didn't like the rain and hoped that it would stop. Me, I didn't mind it, at least not that kind of rain. It was very hot and there had been no rain for about two weeks. The news on telly had been screaming about a drought and how everything was bone dry. This was one of those very heavy showers, the kind that made everything smell fresh and clean. The gutters fill up with fast-moving rainwater that sweeps away all of the accumulated rubbish as it rushes by. The pavements shine and the trees and grass look green again. Even the cars look as though they have just been washed. It's nice. It made me wish that I could have a rainstorm like that in my brain sometimes, to clear out all of the shit in there.

Staggering down the road came Tony's foster father. He was pissed as a newt and trying to sing 'Big Spender' through a mouth that he was obviously having great difficulty controlling.

'Get ready,' whispered Mick and we unhooked the back doors ready to pile out.

'Oh shit,' mouthed Tony nervously.

'Don't worry,' said Mick, 'he can't hurt you any more.'

This bloke was big, but we couldn't stop now.

We had no hassle grabbing him and it was almost like he let us drag him to the back of the now-open van, then he sort of instantaneously sobered up.

'What the fuck!' he yelled and Mick head-butted him in the face. As he fell backwards he threw his arms wide and sent Pete sprawling into the road. His hands were now firmly clamped on to the sides of the van as he tried to pull himself upright. Alan hit him low and hard in the stomach, which on reflection wasn't a good idea, because as he doubled up and pulled his arms in to protect himself, he spewed ten pints of lager out of his now severely bleeding mouth.

'Me strides, look what he's done to me bleeding strides!' yelled Alan and aimed a mighty kick at his balls which made him curl up and roll backwards into the van like a ball.

Seven of us sat on him while Mick slammed the van into gear and wheelspun us away from there. We drove for about twenty minutes and finished up in a car park on Hampstead Heath. The bastard fought all the way.

When we arrived Alan was sitting on his chest, Wivva and me had an arm each, Pete, Den and Tony had his legs and Si, who had stuffed an oil-rag into the guy's mouth, was sitting with his feet on each of the bloke's shoulders while tugging hard with both hands at his hair.

Mick stopped the van, jumped out, ran round and opened the doors and as though at a signal we all pulled at our piece of this guy. We all tumbled out of the van together, arms and legs were everywhere. Mick snapped out orders to each of us and we eventually got him spread-eagled face-up on the ground.

The electricity of the moment was pounding through my body as I dug my knee hard into the side of his neck. He lay quiet, so Mick removed the rag from his mouth. He made to scream so Mick stuffed it back in again quickly and said, 'Make a sound and you're dead.'

The guy nodded as best he could so Mick again removed the rag. This time the guy stayed quiet.

Mick said, 'D'you know why we're here?'

'No,' said the man and he coughed and spat out some blood. After clearing his throat he said, 'If it's money, I ain't got none.'

'No, it's not money,' said Mick. 'This is what it is.'

He beckoned to Tony to show himself.

'What's that lying bastard been telling you,' growled the guy.

'I'm no liar! You know I'm no liar!' screamed Tony as a look of rage spread across his face. The man's eyes widened with terror now that he had begun to realise what was happening.

'What do you want then, boy? Want me to say sorry, eh?' The man gave a bloody grin. 'Okay, okay, I'm sorry, all right now?'

'Not good enough,' said Tony. 'Four years I've taken from you, four long years of shit, filth and pain and you think that sorry is going to be enough.'

'You won't get away with it, you slags,' said the man, trying to sound tough, 'I'll get you, I'll get all of you sometime.'

'We'll just have to make sure that you don't then, won't we,' said Mick and he rammed the rag back into the guy's mouth.

'You first,' we said to Tony.

He jumped and landed on the bloke's left ankle with a loud crunching sound. Si grabbed the wheel-wrench from the van and slammed it against the bloke's jaw, knocking the bottom half of his face sideways. The frenzy then overtook us all. I felt that we must have broken every bone in that slime's body, how he didn't die I will never know. The cassette in the van was belting out Frank Sinatra's 'New York, New York' as we did the business.

Thinking about it now, it must have been one of the weirdest sights that you could imagine. Eight blokes, giving it all to this one bloke and not a sound but the huffing, puffing and grunting as punches and kicks rained down, and over it all, Frankie boy belting out one of his best numbers.

The papers just said that a man had been found severely beaten on Hampstead Heath, it was thought that he had been the victim of a mugging. Funny thing is, we never rolled him. We took nothing off him at all. I'll bet that confused the Old Bill.

Mick drove us back to his place so that we could clean up. Not to his flat in the block where he lives in Hackney, but to the garages underneath, where he used a hose to clean out the van. He then turned the hose on Wivva, me, Tony, in fact the bastard drenched us all. So we jumped on him and stuffed the hose up his trouser-leg. Fucking good water fight that was, went on for over an hour, well, until we saw the blue lights arriving anyway.

Chapter Seven

Sunday morning. Si's uncle Chris had wangled some tickets for a 'Quo' concert at Wembley, so we are all going. Needless to say, Pete and Den were over the moon, at last they were going to see their heroes in the flesh. But first I was to spend the day with Chef and his wife at their place in Greenford.

I had to be there by twelve so I jumped from my bed and grabbed a quick shower and shave. Looking in the mirror I was surprised to see that I had quite a large bruise on the side of my head by my left eye. The centre of the bruise was oozing just a trickle of blood. I must have got caught in the fight and not noticed. That happens often, you get so high that if you do get smacked you just don't feel anything, nothing registers.

I checked the rest of me for any damage. A few bruises on my shins and the skin was gone from both sets of knuckles, but other than that I seemed okay. I stuck a small piece of tissue on my face to dry up the blood and got dressed.

I caught a West Ruislip train at Lancaster Gate and chugged out to Greenford.

Chef lived in a nice little bungalow just down the road

from the station. His front and back gardens were alive with red roses, he was potty about them. I walked up the path and rang the doorbell, then stood back clutching the piddling bunch of flowers that I had bought at the station and braced myself.

The door flew open and this big woman came bundling out and threw her arms around me. She almost crushed every ounce of breath that I had out of me and then planted a massive smacker on my forehead which I knew would leave a bloody great big lipstick smear.

This was Beryl. Beryl was Chef's wife and Beryl was very big, very strong and very, very blonde, out-of-a-bottle type of blonde if you know what I mean. Beryl liked me, thank God. I'd hate to think what she could do if she hated me.

'Stewart darling!' she screeched. I wish she wouldn't call me Stewart, she always calls me Stewart.

'Good to see you, sweetheart, how are you? Oh! You've hurt yourself! Are you all right? Come inside and let me have a look at it. How did it happen? Did someone hit you? Did you fall? Does it sting? You tell me who it was and I'll sort them out. Ooh, it does look nasty. Cheffeee! Come and look at Stewart's face.'

On and on and on she went, but then that's Beryl, her heart's in the right place, it's just that her mouth never seems to stop.

She dragged me into the kitchen and sat me down. She then got some cotton wool, soaked it in Dettol and proceeded to dab at my face. It stung like hell. She finished by sticking an oversized plaster on it and said, 'Now you take care of that or it will fester and go poison.' She then went and put the kettle on for a cup of tea.

Chef had come into the kitchen by this time and stood leaning against the breakfast bar chuckling quietly at my obvious embarrassment.

'Come on, son, I've got some beer in the garden,' he said and walked out of the back door. I followed and still clutching my little bunch of flowers sat down in a deckchair next to his. He handed me a can of lager and looking at the now crumpled posie in my hands asked, 'Were they supposed to be for us?'

I looked down at them and laughed. 'Sorry Chef,' I said, 'she made them go completely out of my head.'

He laughed as he took them and laid them on the ground. 'She has that effect on most people, son, don't worry about it.' He then looked serious and said, 'I see that you were busy again last night. You're going to get into big trouble if you don't watch yourself.'

'What do you mean, Chef,' I said with a grin.

'Don't piss me about, boy,' he said. 'You know exactly what I mean.'

'Sorry, Chef,' I said. And I meant it.

'What happened?' he asked. So I told him. Like I said, I could talk to Chef, he was a bloody good listener.

After I had finished he sighed and said, 'You've got a bloody good head on your shoulders and a natural talent for your work, you could go a long way if you put your mind to it. It would be a pity to see all of that go to waste just because you haven't yet learned how to deal with your past.'

'What do you mean?' I asked.

'Why do you feel the need to keep on doing what you did last night? What do you get from it?'

'I'm getting even,' I said.

'What do you mean by getting even?'

'Just that, Chef, getting even,' I said. 'Stopping those sorts of blokes from picking on innocent kids. Showing them that they can't keep on getting away with it.'

'Are you sure about that?' he asked. 'Some people would see it as mugging, or even queer bashing.'

'I know,' I said. 'I've heard that from people before, but it's not. Last night's was a known nonce. No one believed Tony when he told them what that bastard was like and he could have gone on fostering kids and screwing them for ever, he had to be stopped. The social services couldn't and the police either couldn't or wouldn't, so we did. But it's not queer bashing, not in any way. When those blokes proposition Si at the station, they know bloody well that they are talking to an underage boy, if it was a gay bloke looking for a partner for the night, then there are plenty of places that he can go for that. These blokes are after kids and kids only, they're nonces and they have got to be stopped and if we didn't do it, no other fucker would.'

'That's quite a speech,' said Chef. 'But what happens to you if it all goes wrong? What happens if one of those men goes to the police?'

'They don't,' I said.

'They haven't yet,' said Chef. 'But it could happen.'

'We'll deal with that as and when, Chef.'

'That's daft,' said Chef. 'Bloody daft.'

'What do you think I ought to do then?' I asked.

'I think you ought to deal with your own problems before you start taking on other people's,' he said.

'How d'you mean?'

'Do something about your own father, you're great at

fighting other people's battles and you're good at telling other people that they mustn't let these animals walk free, but yours still is and he's still got your sisters and maybe even a grandchild or two by now. When are you going to do something about him?'

'I can't,' I said.

'Why not,' he said. 'Are you scared?'

'Yes I am, I'm fucking terrified if you must know.' I got up and walked to the other end of the garden.

Chef lit another cigarette and waited. I sniffed and coughed and managed to hold back the tears that I could feel building up. I took a couple of deep breaths, walked back and sat down again.

'Sorry Chef,' I said.

'What for?' he asked. 'There's nothing wrong with getting angry, just so long as you can control it, and there's no shame in admitting that you're scared either. Think about what I've said and maybe you'll begin to understand why it is that you are like you are. As it is, believe it or not, I have a great deal of sympathy and understanding for what you do, I just believe that you are going about it the wrong way.'

We went inside for the biggest Sunday lunch that you have ever seen, all cooked and lovingly prepared by Beryl. Chef never cooked at home. By the time I left, late afternoon, I was full fit to burst.

We were at Wembley by seven-thirty. Pete and Den wanted to make sure of good seats. Si turned up with this bloke who looked like a refugee from the fifties. You know, drape jacket, brothel creepers, elephant trunk hairdo, Elvis sideburns, the whole bit. It was his uncle Chris. He impressed us straightaway by steering us to a side entrance. Then flashing a card at the security guard, he led us straight down to the front of the hall to pick our seats before the crowds came in.

I must admit that my choice of music is a lot slower. Heavy rock and head banging doesn't really do that much for me. But that concert was brilliant. It wasn't so much the sounds, more the atmosphere. Everybody jumped at the same time, everybody rocked at the same time and everybody seemed to know every word of every song. I even caught myself singing along to one or two of the numbers. When they'd finished, the crowd screamed for more. They were just about to go into 'Rocking All Over The World' when Chris told us to follow him and started to push his way through the crowd to the area at the side of the stage.

'Hang on, we want to hear this,' yelled Pete and Den together.

'You will!' screamed Chris back at them, 'you will.'

We got to a line of bouncers who were protecting a double door that led backstage. They glared at us menacingly.

'Oh shit!' I said to Mick, 'what's he doing?'

Chris smiled and produced a wad of cards, one for each of us. He showed them to the bouncers and they moved aside and counted us through, the biggest bouncer saying through a gap-toothed smile, 'Now you behave yourselves back there, lads, or I'll come looking for you.'

'Backstage passes,' mouthed Pete and Den, their faces wide with amazement. 'Backstage fucking passes.'

'How the fuck did you manage that,' I yelled at Chris.

He smiled and said, 'It's not what you know . . .'

'It's who you know,' we chorused.

We watched the end of the show from the side of the stage, Pete and Den's heads were almost totally buried in the massive speakers as they bopped up and down to the beat while strumming their imaginary guitars.

We met the band and were stunned when they invited us back for a drink. We had a jar or four or ten with them and the crew and gave them a hand to pack away all of their stuff. We eventually left loaded with pictures, records, autographs and pissed out of our skulls.

All the way home, the twins swore undying loyalty and devotion to Chris for what they believed was a miracle. I must admit, I thought that the guys were brilliant to treat a load of strange kids like us so nicely; well, they had no need to did they? They could have just told us to piss off, but they didn't. They gained at least one more fan that day.

Chapter Eight

I took Chef's words to heart and for a while threw myself into my work and aimed at getting some qualifications. Chef had pressurised the boss into allowing me two days a week for catering college. I even began to like it, new people around, making new friends, I was getting on well. I still saw the lads occasionally but I had cut down on the amount of business I joined them on. Mick seemed to understand that I had a lot of thinking to do, so he got into the habit of expecting me only when he saw me.

Everything seemed to be going fine. Then Chef died.

I was gutted, destroyed. I loved that bloke, more than he would ever know and the bastard upped and died on me. How could he do that? Didn't he know how much I needed him?

He had just finished preparing a sea bass for serving. It was all tarted up with brightly coloured vegetables, Nouvelle Cuisine he called it. He stood back to admire his work and lit another cigarette. I noticed that he had placed a piece of asparagus in such a way that at first glance it looked like the fish had a giant penis. I pointed it out to him and he started laughing, then he started coughing and then he went. It was as quick as that.

Liz, the kitchen hand, dropped to her knees beside him and started to thump his chest and give him mouth to mouth. It seems that she learned it at one of her Red Cross days. It did no good. As she lifted her head I could see the smoke from his cigarette rising slowly from his nose and mouth.

I stood frozen to the spot, a smile still on my face from the fish joke. I didn't know what was going on, couldn't take it in.

'Call an ambulance!' barked Liz.

I just stood there.

'Stu, call a bloody ambulance!' she screamed again.

I clicked into gear and rushed to the phone.

The ambulance arrived ten minutes later. Liz was still pounding on Chef's chest. One of the ambulancemen gently moved her to one side, while the other checked Chef for a pulse. On finding nothing he began to do all of the things that I guess they do at times like that, then he looked up and said, 'I'm sorry, there's nothing we can do, he's gone.'

Liz cracked up then and had to be led away by one of the other women. I was numb. I helped them to pick him up then took hold of his hand. He was still clutching his lighter. I gently prized it from his grasp and slipped it in my pocket, I've still got it, it's only a grotty old Clipper but it's my most prized possession. Then they took him away.

I didn't go to the funeral, I couldn't face it. I sent the biggest bunch of roses that I could afford with a card that said, 'TO DAD, IF ONLY. LOVE STU'.

I went to see Beryl some time later, she gave me a hug and cried a lot, she remembered the roses and understood the card. I didn't know then that I'd be seeing her more often, for different reasons.

That weekend I went out with the lads and did some business.

Chapter Nine

We've got a new chef now, he's okay, but it can never be the same.

It's one o'clock in the morning, it's very hot and I was sitting just outside the window of my room looking through the railings that run all the way around the roof of the hotel.

I'm watching the 'toms' at work in the square below. Toms are prostitutes, for those that don't know, but I haven't quite worked out yet how cockney rhyming slang turns prostitute into tom; I'll let you know if I do.

She was back again, wearing a tight-fitting red dress that shows all of her legs and sets off her long blonde hair a treat. She doesn't seem to be like the other girls. She doesn't walk to the cars that cruise by, or laugh and joke the way that the others do. If someone wants her, she's always taken to them by one of the other girls. She never seems to smile and rarely talks. If she gets into a car, she's always back within the hour. There was something about her that was bugging me.

I watched for another hour or so until I saw a long dark car pull up and take her away. It was the same car that brings her when she works the square, so I assume it's her pimp. I went to bed.

The following night I started watching earlier. She arrived in the car at about eight o'clock, same red dress, same quiet, almost depressed manner. She stood by the gate to the gardens in the middle of the square clutching her handbag and staring at her feet. I decided to go for a walk.

I walked out of the door of the hotel and across the road towards her, she had her back to me. One of the girls with her said, 'Hello darling.'

I smiled and walked past. I turned to go into the gardens and glanced at her face, her eyes met mine and for an instant the world stopped. Her jaw dropped as she recognised me.

'Stu?!' she said. 'Is that you?'

'Yes,' I said, frowning.

'It's me, Stu, Jenny.'

'Jen,' I said. 'It can't be.' Jen is my sister, she was a skinny eleven-year-old when I left home, but this, this was a young woman. Suddenly, recognition hit me like a brick full in the face. We threw our arms around one another and hugged and hugged. I had a million questions to ask her, but I didn't know how to start. I was speechless, she was sobbing.

One of the older girls walked over, Jen looked up at her and whispered, 'It's my brother, I've not seen him for years.'

She smiled and said, 'Okay, love, but don't be too long. If you're not here when he comes back, you know what'll happen.'

'Thanks, Sally,' said Jen and we started to walk towards the hotel.

'No, not there,' she said. 'It's too close.'

'Okay,' I said, 'come with me.' I took her down the side of the hotel to the car park.

'Hang on a sec,' I said and I ran in the back door, through the kitchen to the chef's office and took the van keys from the hook by the door. I ran back out, grabbed Jenny by the hand and pushed her into the small Escort van that we use for the meat-market. I jumped into the driving seat, started the engine, slammed it into gear and sped off.

I drove out to a pub that I know in Chiswick over-looking the river. Parked up, bought a couple of drinks and we sat looking at the boats.

'What happened?' I asked.

'It was Dad,' she said. 'He got worse and worse, used to bring his friends in to do us while he watched. He got fed up with us, bored he said. Started to call us names like slag and whore, he put Ali in hospital when he thought that she had enjoyed one of his friends too much.'

Ali is my older sister Alison.

'She's still in there. He broke her arms and ribs and ruptured her spleen. She's in a terrible state, I don't dare go and see her.'

'Which hospital?' I asked.

'The Whittington,' she said. 'But don't go, if he catches you, he'll kill you. He's mad, out of his head.'

'Don't worry,' I said. 'I know what I'm doing. Now what about you?' I asked. 'Why are you out here?'

'He sold me,' she said.

'W – w – what?!' I stammered.

'He sold me. He got fed up with me, I got too old for him and he sold me.'

'How? Who to?'

'Someone that he met through his dirty film club, a bloke named Gus. He gave Dad a thousand pounds for me and takes kids to him when he needs them. I've been with him for about three weeks now, he's an evil bastard, he hurts me, Stu, I can't walk sometimes.'

'Okay, babe,' I said and slipped an arm around her as she started crying again.

'I've got to sort this,' I said, 'I've got to sort this. First I've got to get you safe.'

'You can't,' said Jen. 'I've got to go back, if I don't Gus will have me burned.'

'No, he won't,' I said. 'Trust me, I left you once, I'm not going to let you down again.'

We got back into the van and I drove out to Greenford.

We arrived at Beryl's at about eleven o'clock. I rang the bell and waited with my arm protectively around Jen. I felt terrible.

Thousands of things were going on in my head and I needed time to sort them out. Beryl opened the door, saw me and beamed, then she looked at Jen's tear-stained face and pulled us both inside.

'What's happened, love?' she asked. Looking at Jen, she said, 'Who's this lovely thing and why so sad?'

While Jen used the bathroom I briefly explained the situation to Beryl, and before I could ask she said, 'Of course she can stay here, I'd love the company. Now don't you worry, you go and do what you have to do.'

I promised her that I would get some money to help with Jen's keep.

'Don't be silly,' she said. 'Chef left me well-provided for, I've got money coming out of my ears. Anyway, you know very well that Chef would want me to do this.'

I thanked her and gave her a hug.

Jen came back and I told her what the plan was. Beryl helped by explaining that she wouldn't let her out of her sight and that she was perfectly safe as no one but the three of us would ever know where she was. She then made Jen laugh by flexing her muscles and saying, 'And if anyone is fool enough to try, then they will have to walk over me first.'

I kissed them both and left.

I was back at the hotel by one in the morning. I parked up the van and walked over to the staff entrance. It was pitch black. I was trying to find the keyhole when I was grabbed from behind and slammed against the door. A hand pushed my face hard into the wood and a voice said, 'Where is she?'

'Who?' I asked, trying to sound innocent.

'Don't fuck with me,' said the voice.

'I don't know what you're talking about,' I said.

'The red dress, where's the girl?' he said and something whacked across the back of my legs.

'Honest . . . I . . . I don't know what you mean,' I said, trying hard to control the pain.

He spun me around and shoved a knife under my nose. 'Your name's Stewart, her name's Jenny. She's your sister and you took her tonight. Sally told us . . . eventually.'

I heard a chuckle off to my left. Sally, I remembered, was the girl who let Jen go with me. I wondered what they had done to her.

'What do you want?' I asked.

'I want to cut your throat,' said the voice and the chuckler started again.

'Where . . . is . . . she?' he growled.

'I . . . I . . . don't know,' I stammered.

'Oh well, your loss,' he said. 'Say ta ta to your knees.'

A figure loomed up in front of me, he had what looked like a baseball-bat in his hands. Just as he raised it above his head, lights flooded the car park. I screwed my eyes shut and gritted my teeth preparing myself for the pain that I was about to feel. Just then the door behind me began to move.

'I'll be back,' hissed the voice and he disappeared.

I fell backwards into the arms of the night porter and passed out.

I awoke on the settee in the manager's office. I was shaking like a leaf and the backs of my legs hurt like hell. The night porter had dragged me in there before deciding what to do. He gave me some water and asked me if I wanted to call the police.

'No . . . no . . . erm . . . don't call them,' I said. 'I'll be okay.'

'You sure,' he said. 'Those people didn't sound too nice.'

'Yeah, it's okay,' I said. 'It was just a misunderstanding. Thanks anyway, Sam.'

'Okay,' he said, 'it's your life. But if the guvnor hears about this, he's not gonna be any too pleased.'

'Don't worry, Sam,' I said. 'It won't happen again, sorry to have bothered you, mate.'

'No bother to me, mate,' he said. 'You just livened up an otherwise boring night.'

'Thanks, Sam,' I said again. 'I think I'll go up to bed.'

I got up and walked, no limped, to the lift, my legs felt like they were on fire. In my mind the voice hissing 'I'll be back' was playing over and over again.

I got to my room, dropped my jeans and checked the backs of my legs. Straight across both calf muscles and curving round to the outside of my right one was one massive great vivid blue and red bruise. I thought that I was lucky not to have two broken legs.

I went to the pay-phone in the hall and called Mick. I spoke to him for a few seconds, went back to my room and threw a few things into a bag. Then I wrote a short note and pinned it to the back of my door. I climbed through the window, took a long look down at the square, moved around to the side of the building and shinned down the fire escape to the first floor and waited.

Ten or fifteen minutes later a battered old Toyota pulled up outside. I slid down the last few feet, crouched and listened for a couple of seconds, then scurried still crouching to the car.

'Fucking hell,' said Mick. 'What have you been up to now?'

Chapter Ten

I stood by the monument to Dick Whittington and his cat on Highgate Hill, just down the road from the hospital. I was waiting for eleven o'clock and keeping a sharp lookout for anyone that I might know. I had rung the hospital earlier and had been told by the ward sister that I could see Ali for just ten minutes as I was her brother, but I had to wait until the doctors' rounds were over, and they finished at eleven.

I was being ultra-careful because it seemed sensible to me that the evil bastard that had jumped me at the hotel could well have gone to my old man and between them they may well have sussed that I would come here.

It was eleven. Everything seemed okay, so I slipped into the hospital. Ali was a mess. Her face was one big bruise. There was a tube coming out of her nose and another from under the bedclothes about halfway down. That one emptied into a clear plastic bag hooked to the side of her bed. The bag was half-full of blood-stained piss. Both of her arms were in traction and the fingernails on both hands were black and inflamed. Her throat rattled with phlegm as she breathed and her blackened and swollen eyes were twitching as though some kind of insect was under her eyelids scurrying about.

I sat down beside the bed and softly called her name. She caught her breath for a second. I called again and this time gently placed my hand on her shoulder, I felt her pull away. I again whispered her name and this time she opened her eyes.

I gasped. I saw a Dracula film once where Christopher Lee's eyes had turned blood red, and as he died, tears of blood streamed down his face. I remembered laughing. But this wasn't Dracula, this was Alison. I couldn't bear it, I had to force myself to look at her. As she opened her eyes a pool of blood collected in the corner of each as she strained to see who it was that had awoken her.

'Hi, Ali,' I said softly, 'it's me, Stu.'

'Stu, is it really you?' she whispered.

'Yes, toots, it's really me,' I said. I had a massive lump in my throat and was finding it hard to control myself.

She smiled as best as she could and said, 'It's you all right, toots indeed.' I always used to call her toots when I wanted something.

I didn't ask her how she was, that was bloody obvious, so I said, 'Jen's safe, I've got her.'

'Thank God,' she said and breathed a long sigh of relief.

'I'm going to get him, Ali,' I said.

'You can't, you don't know, he's . . .'

'He's what?' I asked, 'he's what?'

'You just can't,' she mumbled with resignation.

'Course I can and I will.'

'Please don't, you don't understand,' she said.

'Understand what?' I asked. 'The slag can't get away

with this.'

'Look Stu,' she said. 'Just take care of Jen, I don't matter any more, just forget it and look after Jenny and yourself.'

'Forget it!' I exclaimed. 'You know I can't do that. What else is there Ali? There's something you're not telling me.'

She went very quiet and started to weep softly.

'He's got my baby,' she said quietly.

'He's got what?'

'My baby, he's got my baby,' she said again between sobs.

'What baby?' I asked. I was gobsmacked.

'I had another one. A little girl, her name's Cheri, he chose that too,' she said and sobbed softly. 'I don't know what he'll do with her, she's only three.'

'Right!' I said. 'That's enough. I promise here and now that you will never have to worry again, I'm going to sort it.'

'Not the police,' she said. 'They messed it up last time.'

'No,' I said, 'not the police.' My mind was in overdrive. The sister told me that I had to go. I kissed Ali gently on the cheek and left.

I was mad, so fucking mad that it hurt. I ran down the stairs barging past everyone in my path and out of the hospital. I ran up the hill to the church on the corner. In front of the church was a giant crucifix with a figure of Jesus nailed to it.

'I thought you fucking protected kids!' I screamed as I ran past and into the park. I stopped at a pile of rubbish bins and kicked fuck out of them screaming, 'Bastard! Bastard! Fucking lousy stinking bastard!' at the top of my voice. I had to get that parasite out of my system, out of our lives. I fell to my knees and blubbed. The people watching must have thought that I had escaped from a nuthouse or something.

I put the phone down after checking with Beryl that everything was okay. I left the phone-box by Archway Station and jumped on a bus to Highbury. There I changed for a bus to Hackney.

I got to Mick's place at about two and pushed open the door. Waiting for me inside was Mick, Wivva, Pete, Den and Alan. Tony was on his way with Si. Mick had already updated everyone and they were all keen to help.

None of us underestimated the problems this time. Not only did we have to get even with my old man, we had to get Cheri to safety and protect Jen and Ali from Gus and his goons. This one was going to keep us all very busy.

When the others had arrived we got down to making plans.

'We all ought to see the old bastard first,' said Mick. 'Just so as we know what we are dealing with.' Everyone agreed.

'That's no problem,' I said. 'At nine o'clock tonight he'll be in his local, just like every other night.'

'Right,' said Mick. 'That's where we'll be going then.'

'What do we do about the others?' asked Wivva. 'How are we going to find them? Do we just sit up at Stu's place and wait?'

'No,' said Mick. 'This time we've got to be clever, very clever.'

'How do you mean?' I asked.

'We are going to have to kidnap the slag,' said Mick. 'And then we are going to get him to tell us everything that we need to know. After we've got everything that we want from him, we are going to have to make fucking sure that he never bothers anyone ever again.' Mick sat back and looked intently at everyone's face. Then he added, 'And you all know what that means don't you?' Everyone was quiet.

'You saying that we've got to top this geezer?' asked Pete.

'Maybe,' answered Mick.

'That's a bit heavy innit?' said Den.

'I know, but there may be no other way,' said Mick.

'There's gotta be,' I said. 'We can't just kill him . . . can we?'

'Well, we could always cut off his feet and hands, cut out his tongue and blind him,' said Mick sarcastically. Then he added seriously, 'We may not have the choice Stu. We can't have him telling anyone, showing anyone, or writing it down, can we?'

'S'pose not,' I said, 'but I've got nothing to lose, I can't ask you guys to do this.'

'Who's asking?' said Mick. Then turning to the rest he said, 'How many of you are in?'

They all punched the air.

Chapter Eleven

We arrived at his local, just down the road from the YMCA at Crouch End, at about eight o'clock that night. We managed to get a booth to ourselves. They plonked me in the corner, got in some drinks and sat themselves down in such a way that I was completely covered. All I had to do now was point him out when he came in.

Wivva tried to cheer us all up by cracking some of his stupid jokes. Didn't work though. He then surprised us all by asking us what we thought about the Iraqi invasion of Kuwait. We all sat open-mouthed.

'What!' he said. 'What's up with you lot?'

'You *read* the papers,' said Mick.

'Course I do,' said Wivva with a pained expression. 'And what's more, I'm gonna join up.'

'Join the Army?' I asked, my face wide with amazement.

'Too right,' said Wivva. 'There's gonna be a battle and if there's gonna be a battle I want to be there.'

'What if they send you to Ireland?' asked Mick.

'No chance, I won't go,' said Wivva. 'I'll tell them to stuff it.'

Good old Wivva I thought, he'll never change. Mick emptied a packet of crisps over Wivva's head as the rest of us creased up.

'Hold it down, lads,' said the landlord.

'Sorry, chief,' said Mick.

He came in at nine-fifteen and sat on a stool at the bar. He hadn't changed much I thought. The same greasy, stringy hair, the same nicotine-stained stubble. He was a bit greyer than I remembered and had a new pair of glasses perched on his beak like nose. But there was no mistaking him, he was still the same five feet, four inch piece of skinny shit that I had run away from all that time ago. I nodded to Mick and pointed him out.

'It's amazing innit,' said Mick. 'Look at the size of that bloke, if anything, a stiff wind would blow him over, but he ruled the fucking lot of you didn't he? You have to wonder how they do it, don't you?'

I nodded, I was feeling really scared.

'Right, watch this, lads,' said Mick, then he got up and went into the Gents.

Two minutes later, he came out and walked over to the bar. He stood next to my old man and ordered a pint of lager. He then nudged the old man's elbow as he was about to take a drink from his glass and made him spill it down himself.

'Shit! I'm sorry,' said Mick. 'Here, let me buy you another one.'

'No harm done,' said my old man, 'mine's a bitter.'

Mick ordered it and started a conversation with him. They were talking for a long time.

A few pints later the old man went to the Gents. Mick motioned to us and we all left. We piled back into the van and went back to Mick's. He said nothing at all until we got there.

Mick smiled and said, 'Stu, your old man is a prat. Everything we need to know about him he told me tonight. It's gonna be a piece of piss lifting him.'

'What'd he say then?' I asked.

'Right,' he said. 'One, he leaves the kid on her own every night when he goes to the pub, the neighbour just listens out for her. Two, he normally gets legless before he staggers home. Three, he's taking his beloved grand-daughter back home to her mother in Brighton this weekend. He said that he will miss the little cherub.'

'But . . .' I said.

'Yes, I know,' said Mick. 'If Mum's in hospital, where's he taking the kid and what's going to happen to her?'

'We are going to have to move fast,' I said.

'Right,' said Mick. 'We lift the bastard on Friday. Now then, where do we take him?'

'Shanks,' said Wivva.

'What?' asked Mick.

'Shanks. It's a factory just off Hackney Marshes. It was shut down about two months ago, my old lady used to work there. It's quiet and safe.'

'Nice one, Wivva,' said Mick, 'Friday then guys.' Everyone nodded.

Wivva thought that we ought to celebrate, so he conned Tony and me into going with him to get some booze and takeaways. We took the van and drove to Dalston to the Pie and Mash shop, best in the country I tell you. With enough pies, mash and liquor to fill three carrier bags we got back to the van and drove to an off-licence. One bottle of rum, one of whisky, a case of

Carlsberg Special, four litres of Coke and we're set for a good night.

We got back to the van and were just about to climb in when we noticed a rumble going on over the road. Four skinheads were laying into a little Asian kid.

'Oi!' yelled Wivva, 'leave him alone, you wankers.'

One of them threw a bottle at us and we ducked as it smashed on the side of the van.

'Right, you've fucking asked for it now!' yelled Wivva as he grabbed the wheel-wrench from the van and charged across the road into the middle of them scattering them like skittles. Tony and me ran over to join him. We tore into them kicking, punching, spitting and scratching, they didn't know what had hit them. We kept on until all four of them had run away so fast that you couldn't see their arses for dust.

The little kid just vanished as we stood and shouted abuse at the big brave skins hobbling and staggering out of sight. We turned back to the van to see the kid come out from behind it and run as fast as his little legs could carry him down the road.

'Poor little fucker,' said Wivva as he climbed into the van. 'He must have been terrified, look at him go.'

'Oh he's terrified all right, Wiv,' said Tony, looking in the box behind the passenger seat, 'he's nicked your fucking rum.'

'What!' yelled Wivva as he lifted out a can of beer and checked for himself. He jumped from the van and chased after the kid, only to give up after about fifty yards. He threw the can after him but it crashed harmlessly to the ground some twenty or so yards further on, spraying beer into the air.

'Little git . . . shit . . . git,' he was muttering to himself as he got back to the van and climbed in. Tony and me were in hysterics.

We looked a right mess when we got back to Mick's but we loved every bit of it. It seemed to round off the day just right.

Chapter Twelve

Friday came. It was about five forty-five and we were all watching *Neighbours* on Mick's telly in his front room. Takeaway pizza boxes and beer cans littered the floor. We were all extra nervous. I'd done specials before, but I was shitting bricks at the thought of this one.

The plan was simple, almost too easy. Mick will be in the pub, wait for the old man and get him talking again. Alan, Tony and Wivva will be there too. I'm to wait with Pete, Den and Si for him to leave home. As soon as he's gone into the pub, Si and me are going to go in and get Cheri. Pete and Den will keep watch. Once we've got her, me and Si take her in Mick's Toyota to Greenford and Pete and Den join Mick and the others. When I've dropped Cheri off at Beryl's, we bomb it back to the factory on Hackney Marshes. If we're late, no problem, they should already be there. If early, fine, we can prepare things for their arrival.

Mick, for his part, reckons that he can chat the old bastard into going for a drive with him in the van to a very special stag night that he knows about. As his life is ruled by the feelings that he has below his belt, I was sure that Mick would have no problem with that. If on the other hand it didn't work, then they'll slug him and bung him into the back of the van.

Neighbours had finished and it was time to go.

Mick, Alan, Tony and Wivva left first. I followed on with Pete, Den and Si. We drove to Crouch End.

As Mick parked up by the side of the pub, I drove on a little further and stopped a few doors down from the house on the opposite side of the road. We then sat back and waited.

We didn't have to wait long. Almost on the dot at nine he came out, leaned over the wall and rang next door's bell. Old Mrs Simmonds came to the door. We heard her say, 'You off then, Tom? Well, have a nice time and don't worry about the kiddie.'

He waved and strutted off down the road. Pete followed him to the corner and waited for him to go into the pub before trotting back and saying, 'All clear boss.'

Si and me got out of the car and walked over to the house. I took out my key, hoping that it still fitted.

It didn't.

'Shit!' I said. 'He's changed the fucking locks.'

'What are we going to do?' asked Si.

'No sweat,' I said, as I stepped over the wall and rang on Mrs Simmonds's doorbell. Si went to go back to the car.

'Hold it, Si,' I said. 'There's no problem, honest.'

Mrs Simmonds opened her door.

'Yes,' she said. 'Who is it?'

'Hello, Maisy,' I said. 'It's me, Stu.'

'Hello, boy,' she said grinning, 'I haven't seen you for ages, how are you?'

'I'm fine thanks, Maisy, how are you?'

'Ooh, mustn't grumble you know. How's Jenny and

Alison? Your dad says that you're all living with your granny in Brighton now, nice Brighton is, I went there once you know, are you anywhere near the beach?'

I swallowed hard, the bastard had covered everything.

'Yeah, not far from the beach, Maisy, you'll have to come down some time, I'm sure the girls would like to see you.'

'Ah, that is nice of you, I'd like that. Anyway, what can I do for you, love?' she said.

'I was supposed to pick up Cheri at five o'clock to take her home,' I said. 'But my motor broke down and now the old man's gone out and I can't get in.'

'He didn't say anything to me, Stu,' she said. 'But then again he's not noted for his memory is he?'

'No,' I said. 'He'd forget his head if it weren't screwed on.'

She gave out with a cackle-type laugh.

'Can you lend me your key for a second, Maisy, I'd like to get her back to her mum before it gets too late.'

'Course you can, love.'

'Cheers, Maisy,' I said. 'And if you can tell him when he gets back that I made it after all, I'd be grateful.'

'Ooh, I don't think that I'll be seeing him tonight, love,' she said. 'You know what he gets like on a Friday night, I doubt he'd notice. Anyway, between you and me, if you don't mind me saying so, I'm glad that you're taking the kiddie home, she's not happy here, always crying.'

'Thanks, sweetheart,' I said. 'I'll bung the key back through the letterbox when I've finished, bye now.'

'No, you leave it on the hall table,' she said. 'With the baby gone, I don't need it any more. Take care and give my love to the girls. Bye bye, darling,' she said and went in and shut the door.

I opened the door and me and Si walked in. It stank of

stale tobacco and booze. I felt terrible. I was shaking like a leaf and the hairs on the back of my neck were standing up. I could feel that shitty bloke all over that shitty house.

'Let's find her and get the fuck out of here,' I said.

We started to check the rooms. She was in the bedroom, in a cot in the corner. We couldn't miss her, she needed changing and the smell was breath-stopping.

'I'll see to her,' said Si. 'I change my uncle's kids all the time when I'm there. You start packing.'

I was grateful to him for that. I didn't want to see what I thought I might, if you know what I mean. He said she was awake, but that she looked frightened. He finished changing her, then he wrapped her in a blanket and hugged her tightly.

I looked around and pulled a big suitcase down from the top of the wardrobe. It was heavy, so I unlocked it and tipped the contents out on to the floor. It was full of magazines, hundreds of magazines and every one of them had pictures of kids being screwed. I felt sick.

'Burn 'em,' said Si.

'No time,' I said. 'Let's just get out of here.'

I threw as many baby things as I could into the suitcase and forced it shut. We started to leave.

'Hang on a minute,' I said and went back to the wardrobe.

'What're you doing now?' asked Si.

'Just watch,' I said as I moved the wardrobe out from the corner and pulled up the carpet. Underneath was a loose floorboard. I lifted it up and took out a biscuit tin. It felt heavy.

'Let's go, Si,' I said as I stuffed the tin under my arm and grabbed the case.

Pete and Den got out and walked down to the pub.

'See you later, guys and don't be late,' they said as they left.

Si got into the back with Cheri as I threw the case into the boot. I jumped into the car and drove off.

Through Crouch End Broadway and up Hornsey Lane to Highgate Hill. I cut a left, down the hill a bit, then turned right into the hospital and stopped.

'Hang on a sec,' I said to Si as I jumped out and ran to the reception desk.

'I've got an urgent message for one of your patients,' I said to the security bloke. 'Could you please give it to the ward sister for her?'

'Sure, son,' he said as he took the envelope from my outstretched hand.

'Cheers, mate,' I said as I turned and zoomed back to the motor. The note said: 'No sweat Toots, Cheri's home and safe. Luv Stu.'

I drove back up the hill and down the other side to the North Circular, followed it all the way round to Hanger Lane, turned right at the roundabout and up into Greenford.

Jen was waiting at the window as we arrived and came rushing out.

'Was it okay?' she asked.

'Fine,' I replied.

She took Cheri from Si and carried her inside, Si and me followed with the case and biscuit tin. Beryl was in the kitchen. She had just finished pouring some boiling water into the teapot.

'I reckon that you can do with one of these darling,' she said.

'Sit yourselves down and I'll get some cups.'

'Cheers, Beryl,' I said. 'You're a life saver.'

I introduced her to Si and we sat down.

'How's the kiddie?' she asked.

'I don't know,' I said. 'I haven't had time to even look at her yet.' It was then that I realised that Cheri hadn't made a sound since we'd picked her up.

'Jen?' I said, looking over at her. Cheri was sitting on her lap trying to hide her head in Jen's chest.

'She seems okay,' said Jen. 'Just a bit frightened.'

'Thank Christ,' I said. 'I thought for a minute there that he had . . . that she was . . . well, you know.'

'Yeah, I know,' said Jen hugging Cheri tightly.

'My sister's a district nurse,' said Beryl. 'She only lives up the road. I'll get her to pop in tomorrow and give the kiddie the onceover.' She looked at my face and added, 'Don't worry, darling, she can be trusted.' I smiled at her and nodded.

I opened the suitcase and Beryl started going through the stuff that I had thrown inside.

'We're going to have to get her some more things,' she said. 'Nappies, though I would have thought that she would have been well out of those by now. Clothes, talc, shampoo, you know, bits and bobs.'

'No need to worry about paying for them,' I said, 'I've got enough here.'

'Jesus, that's his tin,' said Jen.

'Yep,' I said. I had opened the tin and it was crammed full of notes.

'You count it,' I said. 'We've got to go.' Si and me said our goodbyes and left.

Chapter Thirteen

When we got back to the pub, the van was gone. I gunned the engine and we raced to Hackney.

I drove around to the back of the old Shanks factory and saw Mick's van parked by the loading-bay doors. I stopped and we got out. Next to the doors was a large broken window, blood was on the sill and running down the wall. We heard noises coming from inside, so we climbed through. There was a light coming from a door across the loading-bay area. We walked over quietly.

Inside were the lads. Mick and Alan were talking.

'But you could have killed him,' said Mick.

'Serves the shit right,' said Alan. 'It was a stupid thing to do.'

Lying in the corner on a pile of cardboard was my old man. He was making kind of wailing noises and muttering, 'You didn't need to do that, I was going to do as you said, you didn't need to do that.' The left leg of his trousers was torn and bloodstained.

'What happened?' I asked.

Mick turned to me. 'Hello mate,' he said, 'how'd it go?'

'Triffic,' I said, 'but what happened here?'

'Stupid bastard tried to run, so Alan threw him through the window,' said Mick.

'Fucking brilliant it was,' said Pete. 'Just like Superman.'

'Has he said anything yet?' I asked.

'No,' said Mick. 'I thought we'd wait for you before we got started.'

The old man had become aware of a new voice and fell silent. His glasses were smashed so he couldn't make out any faces, but I felt that he knew who I was. There was no going back now. I moved over to him.

'You know me?' I asked.

'Yeah,' he sneered. Pete and Den tightened their grip on his arms.

'Fucking hell!' he shouted. 'That hurts.'

'That's tough,' I said. 'Now just tell me what I want to know.'

'Bollocks!' he growled.

'Naughty, naughty,' said Wivva and he lightly tapped him on the nose with a club hammer that he'd brought with him.

'Shit! Take it easy,' yelped the old man. 'You could hurt someone with that.'

'Bloody hell,' said Wivva. 'I never knew that. Did you know that, Den?'

'Live and learn, don't you,' said Den.

'You do indeed,' said Wivva. 'You do indeed.'

'Let's make him a bit more comfortable,' I said as I looped a length of rope around his right ankle and tied the other end to the bottom of a storage rack. Tony did the same with his left leg and Pete and Den with his arms to other parts of the rack.

The old man was now completely helpless. He reminded me a bit of a rat that we had pinned out at school for dissection.

'Are we gonna talk now, or are you just gonna fuck about?' I asked.

'You shouldn't talk to your old dad like that, son,' he said. 'You remember what I used to do when you got stroppy.'

'Oh, I remember all right,' I said. 'I've still got the scars and I see you've still got the belt.'

He grinned.

I undid his belt and pulled it from him.

'You couldn't do it,' he said mockingly. I folded the belt in half and whipped it hard across his face.

'All right! All right!' he yelped. 'What d'you want?'

'Straight answers to straight questions,' I said.

'Okay,' he said. 'But just keep that mad fucker away from me.'

He looked over at Wivva. Wivva laughed.

'First some information for you,' I said. 'Jenny's safe.'

'I know all about her, the whore,' he spat. 'Gus is gonna have your balls for that.'

I hit him again. I was stunned that he could still be so arrogant. He shut up.

'Like I said. Jenny is safe and Ali is being looked after and when she leaves hospital both her and Jenny will be living with me; you'll never see them again.'

'That's fine with me,' he said, 'the gutless cows never did appreciate all I did for them.'

He was making us all very angry and the stupid bastard never even saw it.

'About the baby,' I said.

'I never touched her!' he shrieked. 'It wasn't me, I didn't do it!'

I froze, my mouth stopped working, I sensed all of us tensing up.

'Who did?' asked Mick, giving the impression that he knew what the old man was talking about.

'It wasn't me!' he yelled again, then said, 'I let him take her out for the day and when he brought her back, she . . . she . . .'

I looked over at Si.

'Sorry, Stu,' he said. 'There was some blood in her nappy when I changed her, I couldn't tell you. I did tell Beryl though, she's going to get her checked out.'

'Bastard!' I hissed at the old man. 'Who?'

'Gus,' he said. 'It was Gus.' He then started wheezing.

'Where is he? How can I get him?' I asked.

'No chance, he'll fucking crucify me,' he said.

'Now that's a good idea,' said Wivva and produced from his pocket a handful of six-inch nails. 'Always come prepared, that's what I say,' said Wivva. 'No good 'aving an 'ammer wiv no nails is it?'

The old man's eyes widened in terror.

'Come on,' he said, his voice trembling. 'You're not serious are you, boys?'

'Right hand first,' I said. 'That's the one he wanks with.'

Pete and Den spread out his hand as Wivva moved over, placed a nail in the centre of it and raised the hammer. He slammed down hard and drove the nail through his hand deep into the floorboard underneath. The old man screamed.

'Tell me,' I said. 'Where is he?'

'Please,' he moaned. 'Please don't . . .'

I took the hammer from Wivva and moved to the other hand. Wivva tossed me a nail. I placed it in his palm and swung the hammer down hard, the nail bent as it bit deep through his flesh and into the floor. He passed out. I felt nothing for him. No horror, no shock, nothing but intense hate. I wanted him to wake up so that I could start on him again.

'Take a break,' said Mick. Alan produced some cans, we all took one, those that smoked lit up. We sat quiet for about ten minutes. Tony flicked on his portable cassette, my music was on it this time. Chris Rea, 'Road To Hell'. It seemed just about right.

'He's gotta tell us,' I said.

'Let me try,' said Mick as he got up and went outside. He came back with a large red can and started to pour petrol over the old bastard's head and body. Coughing and spluttering he woke up.

'Please,' he wailed. 'Please let me go. I won't tell anyone, I promise.'

'What can you smell?' Mick asked him softly.

'W – W – What,' he spluttered.

'What can you smell?' Mick repeated.

He sniffed and sniffed again. Recognition hit him like a thunderbolt.

'No, no, please, you can't do that!' he screamed.

'You've got something to tell us,' said Mick, raising his eyebrow.

'Okay,' he said, 'okay. It's in a tin I've hidden. There's a diary. Everything you want's in there. Names, addresses, even how much they've paid me over the years. There's money there too. It's yours if you let me go, over ten grand there is, you can live good on ten grand you know. Let me go and I'll take you there, you'll never find it without me.'

Si and me looked at each other and burst out laughing.

'What's so funny?' asked Mick.

'I've got it,' I said still laughing. 'I remembered his little hidey-hole from when I was a kid and I cleaned it out when I picked up Cheri.'

'Well, fuck my old boots,' said Mick. 'After all that. So what do we do now?' He turned to me.

'You guys go outside,' I said. 'I'll finish off in here.'

Mick looked at my eyes, nodded and said, 'Sure mate, come on fellas.'

They checked to make sure that they had left nothing behind and left me with him.

I sat cross-legged beside his head.

'Before I go,' I said, 'there's a few things that I have to say to you. You've done your best to make mine and the girls' lives as miserable as you can and all just so you can get what you want. You don't give a shit about us, you don't give a shit about anyone but you, you don't deserve to live. This is for Alison and Jenny and me. But most of all, this is for little Cheri.' I pulled out Chef's lighter, lit him and left.

Chapter Fourteen

'Fourteen fire appliances fought a blaze at an abandoned factory building in Hackney during the night. The fire, thought to have been started by vandals, gutted most of the three-storey building and spread to heathland adjoining the site. Local residents' spokesman Mr John Poole said, "It came as no surprise. We have been expecting something like this to happen for a long time." He called for the Council and the police to increase their security patrols on sites such as this.'

Beryl turned down the telly and passed me the tin.

'We haven't even looked at it yet,' she said. 'We've been kept pretty busy what with Cheri and everything.'

'How is she?' I asked.

'She's going to be fine,' said Beryl. 'My sister gave her a full going over. She's a bit undernourished and has a rather nasty anal fissure, that's a tear in her bum, but she said that lots of kids get that who suffer from constipation and then strain themselves too much. She's left us some medication for it and some vitamins and tonic. She's also left me a diet sheet so that we can get her weight back up again.'

'But she's so quiet,' I said.

'Not surprising, given the life the poor kid's had,' said Beryl.

'Jen tells me that your father would give her a clump if she so much as opened her mouth. She's just learned, in the nastiest way possible, to stay quiet. Give her some time and hopefully she'll be a bouncing healthy child again.'

'I hope so,' I said. 'I hope so.'

I turned the tin over and emptied the contents on to the table. I picked out the cash and passed it to Jen for counting while I went through what was left. There was the diary. It was a large leather-bound book. I quickly flicked through it then put it aside for later. What was left was an Abbey National passbook which had two thousand, four hundred and thirty-two pounds in it. Stapled to the inside cover in a little envelope was his cashpoint card complete with pin number. That was handy, I thought. There was also a bunch of keys with a label tied to them, a Rolex watch, and it was genuine, a solid gold fob-watch that looked very old, a membership card for a club called Fotojoy UK, and finally, a fucking awful picture of him with Ali and Jen taken when they were obviously a lot younger. I slipped the picture into my pocket out of Jen's sight. I was going to destroy it later.

Jen had finished counting the money and sat back stunned.

'How much?' I asked.

'I can't believe it,' she said. 'He was always so broke. There's thirteen thousand, nine hundred and sixty pounds here. Where did he get it?'

'God knows,' I said. 'But it's yours now, yours, Ali's and Cheri's.'

'I couldn't,' she said. 'What if he wants it back?'

'He won't want it back Jen. He's gone away for good, and won't ever be back. The only decent thing that he ever did, before he left, was to tell me to give you all the money.'

Beryl looked at me in that knowing way that she has, but she said nothing. Then she hugged Jen and said, 'We can do some real shopping tomorrow, sweetheart. You, me and Cheri.' Jen's face lit up, the way that a kid's face should when they get a surprise present. It was great to see her smiling.

'Are you sure?' she asked me.

'Would I lie?' I said, holding my palms up. She playfully tapped my head with a bundle of notes, and laughed.

I said my goodbyes and left, taking with me everything from the tin but the money. I went back to Mick's. I tried the cashcard on the way. It worked. I arrived at Mick's with my arms full of takeaways and booze.

The diary was full of names, addresses and numbers. We found it difficult to understand, but it looked very important. On one page was stuck a leaflet, the heading of which read:

DELIVERY SERVICE
Just order the type and service that you require and
we will deliver it to your door within two hours.
No reasonable request denied.
Why not live out your fantasies.

Underneath was a telephone number and a computer password with a list of compatible computers using something called a 'modem' system.

'What's all that mean?' I asked.

'Seems to me like they're delivering kids like pizzas,' said Mick. 'And what's more, it's all high-tech. That means that it's big money and big people.'

'How big, Mick?' I asked.

'Fuck knows,' he said. 'But we may get a good idea if we check out some of these addresses.'

'I'm game,' said Tony. 'But what do we do with it then?'

'We could send it to the Old Bill,' said Den.

'Not yet,' I said. 'I want to get this Gus geezer first.'

'Okay,' said Mick. 'But what then?'

'I don't know yet,' I said, 'let's wait and see.'

'Whatever we do,' said Mick, 'it's gotta be something very, very, special.' He winked. We all got the message.

Chapter Fifteen

I'd just left Ali, the tube was out of her nose and she was looking slightly better. She was full of questions. I answered as many as I could, as best as I could, leaving out of course one or two of the details that, like Jen, she would be better off not knowing. Jen, Beryl and Cheri turned up while I was there. Jen was more like the way I had remembered her, jeans, T-shirt, no make-up, trainers, she'd even had all of her long hair cut off and wore it now cut short like a boy. She looked great. Cheri was chirpy but hid from me when I said hello to her. Beryl picked her up and tickled her tummy; she chuckled and much to my relief she seemed okay.

They were all talking at once, most of the talk being about Cheri. I felt a bit like a spare part so I thought that I'd shoot off and leave them to it. Before I could go, Jen said, 'We've got something for you, Stu,' and handed me a big parcel and four envelopes.

'What's this?' I asked.

'Open it and see,' said Jen.

I opened the envelopes first, they were birthday cards. I had forgotten that it was my birthday.

There was one from Jen with a stupid-looking frog on

it. One from Ali that she had obviously tried to sign herself. One from Cheri in the shape of a teddy-bear and her hand-print inside, and the last one was from Beryl. In it she had written, 'To Stewart with fondest love, Beryl and Chef.' I started to fill up, I had to get out of there.

'Open the present, Stu, please open the present,' said Jen jumping up and down. I tore the paper off and inside was the most brilliant leather jacket that I had ever seen, it must have cost a bomb.

'I remembered that you always wanted one when you were a kid,' Ali said. 'I hope this one's okay.'

'Are you kidding,' I said, 'it's fu . . .' Beryl scowled at me, 'it's triffic, really triffic.'

I put it on, hugged them all and said, 'I must go, things to do you know.'

Beryl said that she'd walk down with me. I turned to go then spun around and said, 'Oh, by the way chaps, Daddy gave me a Rolex,' and flashed my left arm. Both of the girls collapsed into hysterics, Ali moaning 'It hurts, it hurts' between laughs. Always leave 'em laughing, that's what I say.

Beryl walked with me to the main entrance.

'We need to sit down soon and talk about the future,' she said.

'Are the girls a problem?' I asked.

'No, it's not anything like that,' she said. 'They're a joy to have and I'm happier than I've been for a long time. It's just the long term, we've got to start making plans.'

'You're right,' I said. 'Soon, Beryl, I promise.'

'Okay, love,' she said and added, 'and as for you, I don't quite know what you're up to, although I can make some shrewd guesses. Just promise me that you'll be careful. Those girls have had enough pain.'

'Cross my heart,' I said with an innocent look on my face.

'Now don't mess about, Stewart,' she said sternly.

'Sorry, Beryl,' I said. 'I promise that I'll be careful.'

She stuck another of her lipstick smears on my cheek, ruffled my perfect hairstyle and went back inside.

Mick had been waiting in the car. I climbed in and said, 'Okay, my son, let's go and see what that shitty old man of mine's left in his shitty old house.'

'Nice jacket, sweety,' he said.

'Fuck off, you git,' I said as we drove off laughing.

We could feel that something was wrong as soon as we opened the door. For a start, the lights were on and all of the doors were wide open.

'I definitely didn't leave it like this,' I said. We listened for any noises, but the house was quiet so we silently moved ahead and started to check the rooms. Every room had been turned over.

Downstairs, all of the furniture in the front room had been ripped out and the television smashed in, the carpets were ripped up throughout. The cooker had been pulled from the wall in the kitchen and all of the crockery from the cupboards had been smashed. Corn flakes, tomato sauce, sugar, eggs you name it, everything was spilled on to the floor.

Upstairs was no different, every room had been destroyed. The old man's room was by far the worst. His bed was in shreds. The carpet was piled in the corner on top of the completely smashed wardrobe. Cheri's cot was in pieces, the bedside cabinet unrecognisable, even the floorboards had been ripped up and were strewn all over

the place like a kind of Chinese chopsticks. The word
'SLAG' had been spray-painted on the back wall where
the bed had been and 'YOU'RE DEAD, YOU SCUM' was
sprayed in a long jagged line around the rest.

'Notice something wrong?' said Mick.

'What d'you mean, course I fucking do,' I said.

'No, not the mess,' he said, 'something else.'

'What?'

'Nothing's missing. The video, telly, stereo all
smashed but not taken. Even your sister's jewellery is still
there. This wasn't vandals, it was made to look like
vandals by someone who was looking for something.'

'The diary!' we both said together.

'Let's fuck off out of here,' said Mick. We did, quick.

Chapter Sixteen

The week after that was very busy. I moved in at Mick's, well I say Mick's, but it's really his sister's place. She rented it from the council. She'd lived there with her husband and two kids for about five years when he upped and left her for another woman. She met another bloke with his own house over Finchley way and moved in with him. Mick just took the place over. The council haven't said anything, the neighbours haven't said anything, so what the hell, it beats squatting.

Tony, Si and Alan moved in too. Pete, Den and Wivva stayed all day with us but went home most nights.

We checked out as many of the addresses in the diary that we could and by asking around locally we were gutted to find that many of the people listed were not the sort of people that my old man would usually hang around with. For instance, some of the addresses listed were houses obviously owned by people who had money and power. There were doctors, lawyers, teachers, a local councillor and a senior copper, as well as shopkeepers, bus drivers and those sort of people. But the biggest name by far was that of an MP.

We also checked out the Fotojoy UK membership card.

The address on the back took us down to Croydon. It was a dingy little photo-developing shop that did your photos in twenty-four hours or your money back. We went in and Mick flashed the card.

An old guy behind the counter looked at the card, smiled at us and disappeared into the back of the shop. He returned a few seconds later with a large brown envelope and handed it to Mick.

'I hope they are to your liking, gentlemen,' he said.

'How much do I owe you?' said Mick.

'Oh no, sir, it's all part of the service,' he said, and wished us good-day. We went back to the car and opened the envelope.

Now we'd both seen all sorts of porn photos before and we honestly thought that we could never be shocked, but these were terrible. The envelope contained pictures of kids with men, women, animals, bottles, vibrators, bananas, cucumbers, everything that you could imagine. We drove straight home and burned them. At least, we now knew what Fotojoy UK was.

The last thing to check was the keys. There were five of them, like old-fashioned car keys. The label had a number six on it and was stamped Haringey Borough Council.

'Garages,' said Mick, 'did your old man have a lock-up?'

'Dunno, I don't think so,' I said.

'Ring Jen and ask her,' he said. I jumped to the phone and dialled.

'Bingo,' I said as I put down the phone. 'She said that he took over one of those around the back about three years ago.'

We were there within the hour. Number six had a blue door. One of the keys opened the lock, the door then swung up and over. There was a motor inside covered with one of those big grey plastic car covers. Against the wall were four old filing cabinets. Mick lifted the corner of the car cover.

'Sheeeit! Check this out.' He whipped off the cover and there stood an immaculate Ford Orion 1600 GL, brand spanking new, the road tax still had eleven months to go.

'Where the fuck did he get that?' I said. Mick was already inside checking it out.

'I don't believe this,' he said. 'Come and look, Stu.'

I opened the passenger door and watched as Mick pulled out the contents of the glove box.

'Look,' he said, a look of wonderment on his face. 'The car keys and the fucking log book. Was your old man some sort of prat or something?'

'Whose name's on the log book?' I asked.

'Fotojoy UK,' said Mick. 'It's a company car.'

'He must have worked for them then,' I said.

'Right,' said Mick. 'Seems a pity to leave it here, Stu.'

'Who said we're leaving it? No one knows what's happened and no one's looking for it.'

'That's what I like to hear. It'll be a change driving a motor with a proper tax disc on it instead of a Guinness label.' He laughed.

The other keys fitted the filing cabinets, but I wished they hadn't. They confirmed that he was working for Fotojoy UK. Pictures, pictures and more pictures. Hundreds, no thousands of them, just as bad if not worse than the shit that we had got earlier that day, and all of them in large brown envelopes. I locked them away again, thinking that later they could provide the evidence that the Old Bill might need.

We both felt very sick and very angry. Everything that we had been doing over the years suddenly seemed right. If we had had any doubts, those photos wiped them out completely. No way could we allow people like that to continue.

Chapter Seventeen

'Police today confirmed that the body of a man has been found in the debris of a fire that took place in Hackney during the weekend. It is thought that the man was the victim of a gangland-style execution. A police spokesman said, "We believe that this man was killed by members of his own gang" and dismissed rumours of a war between rival factions of Triads.'

'Wait till they see the house,' said Mick as he flicked the telly off. 'That'll get them buzzing.'

We were all at Mick's planning what to do.

'It's too big,' I said. 'We're out of our league with all this.'

'So what do we do?' asked Den.

'I don't know,' I said, 'I just don't know.'

'Look, all we want is this piece of filth, Gus, right?' said Mick. 'Then what say we just get him and send the rest of the stuff anonymously to the Old Bill. They've got to do something with all that.'

'I dunno,' said Wivva. 'Remember it was me that sussed out that one of the geezers in that diary was a copper, what if he's on the team that we send it to.'

'Good point,' said Den.

'Why not send it to one of those TV investigators, y'know like Roger Cook or that Esther Rantzen,' said Tony.

'They'll sort it.'

'Only if it makes good telly,' said Pete.

'And only if no one in telly is involved,' added Den.

'Hmm, hmm,' grunted Mick. Then he said, 'But you're right Tony, that's what we need, someone we can trust.'

'Okay, like who?' I asked. Everyone fell quiet.

'Chris,' said Si. 'Uncle Chris.'

We all looked at him.

'Well he did all that at the Quo concert for us didn't he, and we did get on well didn't we?'

'True,' said Mick. 'But why would he help us with this?'

'Well a couple of years ago,' said Si, 'he blagged a place out Watford way. When he went through the bedroom he found a stash of H; he hates drug dealers, killed his brother they did. He once said, "Drug dealers and Nonces, they're the scum of the earth." Anyway, he finished the house, then he tipped off the Old Bill. The guy whose house it was went down for five years and no one bothered about the blagging. I'm sure he'll help us get these bastards.'

'Right then, let's go see Uncle Chris,' said Mick.

'No, I'll ring him, he'll come over,' said Si.

Uncle Chris was no div. He had A-levels to prove it. He was thirty-eight years old and worked as an insurance agent knocking on doors and collecting the weekly payments from his customers, supplementing his income with what Si took from us and the occasional blagging. One, maybe two a year was his limit. 'No need to be greedy,' he would say. Sweet as a nut it was.

It was him or his business friends who arranged the insurance for the houses that got mysteriously done, so he always knew, or heard when one was going to be empty for a while. If it was one of his customers that got done, he would always make sure that he was somewhere with a lot of witnesses when the roll took place. Chris was devious, hard too. He also knew a lot of people from a lot of games, which is how he came to get the passes for the Quo concert.

His motor always had Elvis, Chuck Berry or Jerry Lee Lewis banging out at top volume, and he had an absolute passion for Lonnie Donnegan and skiffle. But as I said, he was no fool.

Personally, I wouldn't trust him as far as I could throw him, but he did think the world of Si and that for me outweighed most of his bad points. Anyway, he was one of those blokes that you just couldn't help liking. Bent as a nine-bob note, stickiest fingers in the world, but would do anything for anyone.

He studied the diary for over an hour, making notes on a piece of paper. Then he took a deep breath and said, 'Well boys, let's tell you what it seems you've got here.'

The diary was mind-blowing. We all listened carefully and tried to take in everything that he was reading out.

'Firstly,' said Chris, 'there are full names, addresses and telephone numbers of people that have used Alison and Jen, those are in turn cross-referenced to the person who introduced, or should I say recruited, them and the whole lot is then cross-referenced back to the person running the area. There seems to be nine areas in London, each with its own reference number and organiser. The organiser in this area is this bloke that you are looking for, Gus. His name, address and telephone number are all here.' Chris had drawn a crude diagram to help us to understand that the whole thing was run like one of those pyramid selling schemes.

He went on, 'There's not much information on the other eight, but this book covers Gus's area completely.' He looked up. 'If this book is true, then it is the sickest thing that I have ever seen and it must be stopped.' He flicked to a page and looked at me.

'Stu, Alison and Jen's names are on a list with the names of over two hundred others. Next to each name is a date of birth and a reference number. The reference number ties up with a list on the next page, each number describing a different kind of kid.

'For instance, all of the even numbers are girls and the odd numbers are boys, with different numbers within those for different types of boys and girls – y'know, if they are black or Asian or something. Next to that list is a scale of charges. Every sex act that you can think of is listed here with its own code number and each of those code numbers is again listed with its basic cost beside it.'

He turned the page.

'On this page is contact information. Nine telephone numbers are listed, each of them with their own particular ringing code, you know, ring three times, hang up and ring again sort of thing. Several of the numbers have been scrubbed out and replaced with new ones, one of them four times. So we can safely assume that these numbers are always being changed. At the top of the page is a number that has to be used if there is a problem with any of the other numbers. That one has been changed six times.

'I've made a swift count of the number of times that Ali and Jen have been used and checked that against the basic charges listed. Sorry Stu, but your old man must have made at least twenty grand from those two within the past year alone.'

He sat back and sighed deeply, then he said, 'This book is dynamite. If all of this is true, then I don't doubt that they would kill to get it back. If they know that you've got it, then God help you, or anyone who knows you.'

'What d'you mean by that?' I asked.

'They've already jumped you once,' he said. 'When you took Jen away. You thought they were getting heavy because they had lost some income, but it's not the girl they want, it's what she knows. While she was working for them, they controlled her. Now they don't know what she's doing or saying. Add to that the strange dis-appearance of your old man and the fact that they can't find this book, then it's a fair bet that they are going to put two and two together and come looking for you. If they can't find you, then they'll look for Jen, if they can't find Jen, then they'll go for Ali. It will go on and on until either they find you, or they are stopped. They have far too much to lose otherwise.'

'Why did they leave such an important book with my old man?' I asked.

'Could be a number of reasons,' said Chris. 'Maybe they thought that he could be totally trusted because he was in so deep. Maybe he kept it to protect himself if anything went wrong. He knew that if he tried anything they'd kill him and if he were to take this stuff to the Bill, maybe he thought that he would get a deal, though I'm sure that he would have to go down for what he'd been doing. Anyway, who'd think that a slime like that would have this sort of stuff, he was perfect.

'Then again, maybe Gus didn't keep this book. Maybe it's your old man's. From what you said about his filing system for photos and the like, he seems to like to keep all of his affairs in order, so why couldn't he have kept it for his own use?'

'Sounds likely,' said Mick. 'So what do we do?'

'I agree that it might not be a good idea at this time to involve the police,' he said. 'But that must come sometime. Anyway, you guys have a few problems that I'm sure you don't need the Old Bill knowing about, so when they're dealt with, the Bill will get to know through another party and I've got an idea on that, so I'll check it out and let you know. For now, protect Jen and Ali or they'll get them. I know you've got to do something about this Gus creep and I'd rather not know any of the details, so get it done quick. We can't sit on this shit for too long, it's far too dangerous and I've got a wife and kids to think about.'

I was sure that he also had his pocket to care for; it was obvious, I thought, that he didn't need the police in at this time because he had seen a once in a lifetime opportunity to make a big score. If there was any money to be made, then you could bet that Chris would be at the head of the queue. I made up my mind to keep an eye on him.

Jen was safe, but Ali wasn't, so we went to the hospital the following morning. I went in with Mick while the rest waited outside. After what Chris had told us, we were taking no chances.

I introduced Mick to Ali then briefly explained what

was happening, leaving out the gory details of course. Ali told us everything that she knew about Gus. The man we wanted was about fifty years old, short, quite fat and balding. He kept two minders with him everywhere he went and like him they were evil. He is driven everywhere in a large black Mercedes that bears the numberplate GUS 101. His car is his office. He spends more time in it with his minders than he does anywhere else. He also takes most of his pleasures in the car, she said with a shudder. She begged me to be careful, I kissed her and left.

At the ward sister's office, I asked if she could make sure that no one but myself and Jen visited Ali, and that any mail, parcels or presents delivered for her should be held until I arrived. I then explained that the guy that had beaten her up was her father and that we had to make sure that he didn't try to get to her while she was in there. I also lied and told her that the police had been informed and were waiting until she was stronger before they interviewed her. The sister was very understanding and agreed at once. She also promised not to talk about our conversation to Ali.

We went back to the cars. Mick was driving the Orion, I thought that I owed him that much, with Pete, Den and Wivva. I was in the Toyota with Alan, Tony and Si. We were going to Gus's place.

We turned right out of the hospital and down towards the Archway. Gus lived in Highbury near the Arsenal football ground so the drive was only about twenty minutes. We drove along Holloway Road, past the Nag's Head, under the bridge and turned left after the Poly. We followed the road round to Drayton Park tube station and turned right. Mick slammed on his brakes, I screamed to a halt just behind him missing his bumper by inches. He then drove on for about twenty yards, pulled into a side-street and parked, I followed. He got out and came back to me.

'Didn't you see it?' he said.

'See what?' I asked.

'Back down there, outside the betting shop. GUS 101.'

'Shit!' I said. 'Let's go take a look.'

'No, no,' he said. 'I'll go take a look, they don't know me.' And off he went with Wivva.

They were away for about ten minutes when through my rear view mirror I saw Mick running full-pelt back to the car.

'Start up!' he yelled. 'Get ready to go.' He rushed past and jumped into the Orion.

Wivva came flying round the corner, zoomed up to us, threw himself into the open door of the Orion and they screamed off closely followed by me. In the mirror I could see two big blokes running up the middle of the road behind me.

Wivva was still laughing when we stopped ten minutes later in Finsbury Park. We piled out, keen to know what had happened and sat on the grass. Mick gave us the story.

'Gus was in there putting on a bet,' he said. 'His two boyfriends were with him. I stood beside them reading the sheets while they studied form and talked to each other. He chose a horse, wrote down his bet, nice pen, and as he was going to the window to place it, one of his goons said, "If we don't hurry Gus, we won't get to the hospital before your meet with Danny." Well, Wivva and me thought ho ho, he's going after Ali, so Wivva told me to get back to the motor, start it up and be ready to go, so I did and that's all I know. Wivva knows the rest.'

'It was simple,' said Wivva with a big innocent look on his face. 'I thought I had to stop him going to the hospital, so I lobbed a brick through his windscreen.'

Everyone fell about.

'It was fucking close though,' he said when he came up for breath. 'For big blokes, those two were bloody fast.'

We all collapsed again.

We cruised past his house twice that day. The first time one of his boys was picking bits of glass out of the front seats, and the second, a new windscreen was being fitted by one of those mobile replacement services. But he didn't go to the hospital.

I went back to see Ali that night. The sister stopped me on the way in and said that someone had telephoned to ask how Ali was. She said that she didn't confirm that Ali was there and also that she couldn't give out any information on any patients without knowing who the caller was. She said he wouldn't leave his name and hung up. I thanked her and after a short visit with Ali, I went back to Mick's and we started making plans.

Chapter Eighteen

It was six o'clock in the morning and everyone was asleep except me. The fucking armchair that I had slept in had given me a crick in my neck. Why was it that they could sleep and I couldn't? I thought. I looked at them one by one.

Mick was in one of those chairs that slide back and magic up a foot-rest. His arms were folded across his chest and there was a silly grin on his face. I thought of that advert saying, 'In your dreams you too could be in Tunisia'. I wondered where he was and if she was worth the dream.

Pete and Den even sleep alike, I thought as I looked at them. Even their bloody hair looked like it had been messed up in the same way. They were both on the settee, one at each end. Both had a leg hanging over the side and both had an arm wrapped around their head. I wondered if they dreamed the same dream.

Wivva slept as hard as he lived, never giving anything away. He was sitting in the corner on a big cushion, knees drawn up, arms folded on the top. His head was lying on his arms with his face turned to the wall. The back of his head had a big 'V' cut into his quarter-inch hair – Vinny

Jones was his hero. His knees were spreading the tops of his arms in a way that made it look like his already well-developed muscles were even bigger. Even in his sleep he was saying, 'Don't truck with me man.'

Si was curled up in a sleeping-bag by the fireplace. He was sucking his thumb and still sniffing even in his sleep. He's a kid, just a kid, I thought. I wondered what would be happening to him if we weren't about. To be honest, I think we all saw a little bit of ourselves in Si, you know, that scared kid bit. It was almost as though we needed him to be around, to remind us of what we once were, or still are.

Tony was lying on his stomach by the window, his arms stretched out above his head. His mouth was wide open and he was softly snoring. His eyes were going nineteen to the dozen so the dream he was having must have been very busy. He talked a lot about his mum last night, calling her names like 'slag' and 'bitch', but we all saw that he didn't really mean it. He still loved her lots, but he just couldn't bring himself to admit it.

Alan? Well Alan was just that, Alan. He was always there, just like the furniture. He rarely spoke, never seemed to have an opinion about anything, but he made you feel fucking comfortable when he was around. I looked at him stretched out in his armchair with his feet crossed and his arms clasped across his stomach and wondered if he ever dreamed at all. Then he opened his eyes and looked at me. I smiled and mouthed the word 'Coffee'. He nodded, we got up quietly and crept into the kitchen.

I suddenly realised that I had never really been alone

with Alan and for a second or two wondered why. No answers came to mind.

I poured the boiling water into two cups, Alan got the milk and sugar.

'One or two?' he said, holding up the sugar bowl.

'Two please,' I said. We took the coffee out on to the balcony to drink and looked at the view. We were fourteen floors up and it was amazing.

I asked Alan how he felt about all that was happening.

'Like what?' he asked.

'You know,' I said. 'All this with Jen and Ali.'

'I don't think about it,' he said.

'But I killed my old man the other night,' I said, and it hit me for the first time. 'Fucking hell! I killed him,' I said.

I hadn't thought about it. You crush a cockroach and you don't think about it, it was the same with the old man. Bloody hell, if someone had told me that one day I would top someone and it wouldn't have any effect on me at all, I would never have believed them. But it meant nothing to me, just like the cockroach. He was here and now he's not and I feel nothing.

'I killed him,' I said.

'So what,' he said. 'If you hadn't I would have. So would Mick or Wivva or any of 'em. He was scum, he had to go.'

'And what about Gus?' I asked.

'If it happens, it happens,' he said. 'People like that put people like us where we are and no one seems to give a shit but us. If that's what we've got to do to stop them, then fine, I'm game and so are all of the others. We talked about it when you went to see Ali. If we get caught,' he went on, 'what can they do? Send us down, that's no worse than we've been used to is it? And if we do get caught, we'll be fucking heroes. Bollocks to them, that's what I say. And the sooner they're all out of the way the better.'

I was flabbergasted. That was the longest that I'd ever heard Alan talk and what's more, there was nothing he said that I could argue with.

There was a noise behind us and we turned. Mick was standing in the doorway hugging a can of Special Brew and coughing over his first smoke of the day.

'That goes double for me,' he said between chokes.

Chris arrived at about twelve. He looked very serious as he sat down.

'I spent the whole day yesterday on this bloody book,' he said, 'and it kept me awake all bloody night. Some of these names are very powerful people.'

'We know that,' said Wivva sarcastically.

'Right, but do you know what it means?' said Chris, leaning towards Wivva. Wivva went quiet and we all smirked.

'What it means is this,' and off Chris went.

'Twenty per cent of the people in this book are powerful enough to stop any investigation. If you want to get them, then you have to catch them at it. It's not enough that their names are in the diary, anyone can write down names, but it wouldn't necessarily stand up in Court. I got that from my brief.' He looked up at us. 'Don't worry, he can be trusted. It's just that he's seen too many cases fail because of unsubstantiated evidence.' He went on, 'My brief knows a tame copper. For those that don't know, that's a copper who thinks before he acts. Someone who's not going to barge in regardless, but is willing to wait until the evidence is properly provided. He's also a good friend of my brief.'

He continued, 'Another way to get the evidence we need is to find what's called a weak link. That's someone who's worked inside with them for a long time and is willing for some reason to give evidence against the names in the diary. What I'm saying is, that the diary's not enough on its own if we want to make sure that these bastards go down.'

'Leave it with us,' said Mick. 'We'll think of something.'

'I thought you might say something like that,' said Chris, 'so I brought you a present that I thought you just might need.' He opened up a sports bag that he'd brought with him and took out a sawn-off twelve-bore and a box of cartridges.

'Brilliant!' yelled Wivva. 'Shooters are brilliant, bags I use it,' and he made a grab for it.

'Hang on,' said Mick, taking it before Wivva could get there. 'We'll sort out who uses it and why later.'

'I picked it up when I did the Watford house that Si told you about,' said Chris. 'I thought that one day I'd maybe use it on a proper job, but then what with the new baby and all and the business going so well, it just stayed in the loft.'

'Nice one,' said Mick, 'Thanks Chris, I've a feeling that this could come in quite handy.'

'I don't know what the bloke used it for,' Chris added. 'So make sure if you use it, or if you're stopped, that you don't get caught with it. You don't want all of his shit on you as well. And please, please, take care eh?' He looked very concerned.

'Thanks, mate, we will,' said Mick.

Wivva picked up the gun and started polishing it with his sleeve. 'It's nice Chris,' he said. 'Very nice.'

It was near eight o'clock and we'd just finished yet another takeaway, curry this time. We were getting ready to carry out the plans that we'd been making all afternoon when a terrific bang came from the kitchen and bounced all the way through the flat.

'What the fuck!' yelled Mick as we all piled out of the room and rushed to where the noise had come from.

Wivva was standing by the kitchen window with a look of absolute amazement on his face and the now smoking shotgun in his hands.

'It just exploded,' he said. 'I just pointed at this pigeon sitting on the balcony, pulled the trigger and *bam!* it was gone. Just fevvers, lots and lots of fevvers, hundreds of the fuckers. It was brilliant.' He started to laugh, we all joined him.

'Nothing like starting a new job with a bang,' said Mick as he took the gun and playfully cuffed Wivva around the head.

The phone killed the moment. It was the hospital. Someone had left a parcel for Ali.

Chapter Nineteen

It was a shoebox, wrapped in gold foil, with a big red bow on it. Mick and I took it to one side. I opened it. Inside, lying on the top of a layer of white tissue paper was a card. It read: 'Remember Brighton' and was signed 'Love G'. I lifted up the tissue paper.

Underneath was a used condom and a picture of Gus and his two goons with Ali and Jen. They were all naked. A note with them read: 'Stewart will listen to you sweetheart. If he doesn't, well . . . Brighton was nice wasn't it.' I thanked the ward sister, stuffed the box under my arm and we slipped out without Ali seeing us or knowing that we had been there.

'Bastard!' I growled. 'Fucking stinking bastard!' We headed out to Highbury to meet up with the others.

Tony was at the end of the street by some trees, watching the house as we pulled up.

'His motor came back twenty minutes ago,' he said. 'He's got four blokes with him now. Two of them are sitting in the brown Granada outside.'

'Must be expecting something then,' said Mick. 'Better not disappoint him, had we?'

The others joined us, they'd been sitting in the car

around the corner. We split troops again. Mick took Alan, Pete and Den in the Orion and I had Wivva, Tony and Si.

We cruised slowly past the house making sure that the two outside knew who we were. We carried on around the block. When we turned back into the road again, we saw that the Granada had gone. We tensed, ready for action. 'Looks like this is it,' I said.

Just as I said that the Granada came screaming up on us from behind, headlights ablaze. It roared past me and sideswiped Mick's Orion, slamming it into a parked VW. Mick's engine stalled. The Granada did a high speed handbrake turn and started back. I swung my car hard over to the right as the Granada again spanked the Orion on the side and sped past me; it stopped at the end of the road and started to turn again. I looked at Mick, he was still trying to start his engine.

We heard a loud crunching noise and watched with wonder as the rear door of the Orion was forced open from the inside, ripping up and out most of the metal covering the rear wing. Out stepped Alan holding the shotgun. He stood as calm as could be in the middle of the road facing the oncoming car; he looked massive. I swear his face had a smile on it.

'Charles fucking Bronson or what!' screamed Wivva. It was without a doubt the most exciting thing that I had ever seen. Alan was at that moment, I'm sure, everything that any of us ever wanted to be.

We all began to scream, 'Shoot the bastards, shoot the bastards!'

He fired both barrels and reloaded. The first two shells smashed into the front of the Granada creating clouds of steam. Alan fired again, this time hitting the windscreen.

The nose of the car scraped the ground as the brakes were slammed on and it started to skid out of control. It screeched past me and caught Alan low on the leg spinning him into the air. The car then careered off into a tree and exploded into flames, no one got out.

We ran to Alan who had landed some fifty feet away from where he had been hit. He was a mess. His right leg was twisted crazily underneath his body, blood was pouring from so many places that it was hard to see how best to stop it. Mick was kneeling beside his head, he looked up and said, 'Don't bother, he's dead. His neck's broken.'

We fell quiet.

A screech and a roar came at us from behind, we all turned and dived for cover. The Merc sped past hitting Alan again, smashing him into the kerb, then it roared off down the road.

'After it!' screamed Mick as we all piled into our cars and sped off, Wivva grabbing the gun on the way.

We lost the bastard at the bottom of Blackstock Road.

'He must have doubled back up by the Arsenal,' said Wivva.

We couldn't hang about, we could already hear the sirens of the Old Bill. So keeping to the back streets where we could, we limped home to Hackney. Not a sound was made by any of us. No speaking, no coughing, no moaning, nothing.

Mick was grazed all down his right side. Pete and Den had a few bumps and bruises but were otherwise okay. We were all sitting quietly drinking beer. Wivva, with tears in his eyes said, 'He was a fucking hero, they ought to make a film about him.'

Pete and Den began to talk about the strength he used to open the car door.

'How the fuck he pushed that thing open, I'll never know,' said Pete. 'Then he just winked at us, smiled and got out, we didn't even know he had the shooter until it went off.'

'Great bloke, the fucking best,' said Wivva now openly crying.

Si called his uncle Chris.

'He'll be here in half an hour,' he said and put the phone down.

'I've got to protect Ali,' I said.

'No need,' said Chris. 'She's not important to Gus any more. He may get her when this is over, just to teach her a lesson, but for the moment he's got more than enough on his plate trying to deal with you lot. He only approached her to get to you remember. Now that he knows who you are and probably where you are, he thinks that he can pick you off whenever he wants to. His only mistake so far was in underestimating you all. He thought that he was just dealing with a load of kids, but he was wrong.'

'Too right,' said Wivva.

Chris went on. 'It's likely that he'll sit back for a while to lick his wounds and take stock of the situation, but that doesn't mean that you can relax. He's got to get you all, you still have the book. And even if you didn't have it, you've read it and that makes you all very dangerous to him.'

'So what now?' I asked.

'Now you get careful, very careful,' he said. 'If you're going anywhere in the cars, each of you go a different

way. Don't stay together unless you have to. As for
what you do about Gus? Well you've unnerved him and
he made mistakes when you took the battle to him.
You've got to keep that flowing. Don't let him breathe.
It seems that he has problems if he can't control the
moves.'

'But where do we find him?' asked Mick.

'He'll be back at home,' said Chris.

'Not after what's happened surely?' I said.

'Why not,' said Chris. 'He's got the front and probably
the contacts that can keep him well out of this. After all,
it was something that happened in the street. The
Granada was probably nicked. The goons were hired for
the job, Alan's got form, if he's identified the Bill will
think it's a gang war.'

'But he hit Alan wiv his motor,' said Wivva.

'I know mate and I'm sorry,' said Chris.

'Fucking hell, he's covered every way ain't he,' I said
angrily.

'Yep,' said Chris. 'You don't get what he's got by being
stupid.'

'Let's go get him then,' said Wivva, jumping to his feet.

'Later,' said Mick. 'Let them clean up the street first. He
won't expect us to come back at him tonight.'

'Can we eat then,' said Wivva. 'I'm fucking starving.'

'Good idea,' said Tony. 'Come on, Si, let's go get some
Chinese.'

Si, Tony and Wivva then raced each other down the
stairs – all fourteen floors of them.

'You'll take care of him, won't you?' said Chris.

'Who?' I asked.

'Si – you'll take care of him.'

'Course we will, he's tougher than you think, you know.'

'I know,' he said. 'I wanted to take him home with me but he wouldn't hear of it.'

We were relaxing, winding down a bit when Tony and Wivva came bursting back into the room.

'They've got him!' they shouted together. 'They've got Si!'

Chapter Twenty

The voice on the phone said, 'You've got something that we want, we've got something that you want. I'll ring later and we'll talk trade.' Then they hung up.

'They must have followed us and waited downstairs,' said Tony.

'The car could only have come through the car park. We got to the Chinky's and Wivva and me were ordering, Si went outside for a slash, we heard a motor pull up, a door banged, and it screamed off. We rushed out and the Merc was bombing through the car park and away. We ran straight back here.'

The phone rang again, Mick answered it. After a couple of minutes he put it down and said, 'Tonight, Highbury Fields, right in the middle, three o'clock. Only two of us can go.'

Chris went to the phone as I said, 'You and me, Mick?'

'I think so,' he said.

Chris came back and said, 'Do what you have to, I'll catch you later,' and left.

Me and Mick took the Toyota and got there at two-thirty, we sat back and waited. The others had left before us in the van. The plan was for them to park over the

other side of Holloway Road, come over to the fields one
by one and hide themselves away until they were needed.
We hoped that they were there.

'Fucking hell!' said Mick as a frozen foods delivery
lorry pulled up and parked, blocking our view. 'What a
place for that tosser to pick for an overnight stop.'

We pulled a little further up the road and settled back
again. On the dot of three the Merc appeared.

'I'll go,' I said.

'Together or not at all,' said Mick.

The Merc pulled up on the kerb by the grass some fifty
yards away from us, one bloke got out. Mick climbed out
and looked at him. He nodded and another guy got out.
They started to walk towards the middle of the green. I
stuffed the diary inside my jacket and got out. We walked
over to meet them.

'You got it, kids?' asked the first guy.

'Got what?' said Mick.

'The book, boy,' said the man.

'The book you got off of Tommy,' said the man. 'He
shouldn't have had it and we know that you've got it. So
give it to me and we can all go home.'

'Where's Si?' said Mick.

'In the motor, son,' he said.

'Show me,' said Mick.

'No, book first,' said the bloke.

'No way,' said Mick. 'Si first.'

The guy looked at Mick carefully and said, 'Got it with
you?'

'It's around,' said Mick. I was fucking glad he was
doing the talking.

'In the motor is it?'

'Si first,' said Mick.

'He's around,' said the guy. This was getting fucking stupid I thought. One of us had to break first.

The guy looked over my shoulder and said, 'It's not in the car then?'

'Who says?' said Mick.

'He does,' said the bloke and nodded towards our car. We turned and saw a geezer standing by the open driver's door shaking his head, two more were walking towards us.

'Open the jacket, boy,' he said to me and reached out. Mick grabbed his arm and twisted, the bloke just shrugged him off and he fell on his back.

Then all hell let loose. Suddenly, as though they had been down holes in the ground, the other boys jumped up screaming and piled into the two guys with us. They'd been lying on the grass, in the dark all this time and no one had seen them.

The three other blokes came at us from behind, tearing into us. I caught something from one of them across the face, dunno what it was, but it felt that it had taken half my face away. I was numb all over the left side. I staggered and fell back.

'Leather jacket! Get the one with the leather jacket!' one of the goons yelled and two blokes jumped at me. I tried to scramble away thinking to myself, we're getting caned, we've had it, they're gonna kill us. Mick slammed me to one side and threw himself at the goons that were after me. They all fell in a heap.

Two more motors came screaming on to the grass, their headlights smashing the darkness to pieces. They skidded to a stop and blokes piled out of them.

'Run!' I screamed. 'There's more of them!'

But we couldn't. They had us. I took out the diary ready to give it up.

The new blokes came hammering over towards us, bye bye world I thought. But they started to tear the goons apart. We couldn't believe it. We sat and watched in amazement as they pole-axed one, then another. Bodies were all over the place.

One of Gus's blokes managed to get back to the Merc and start it up, the guy next to me let out a loud screeching whistle. The frozen foods lorry that had blocked mine and Mick's view earlier started up, slammed into gear and shot forwards towards the Merc. It smashed into its front, stopping it dead, the guy inside came flying through the windscreen.

'Nice one,' said a voice next to me. I turned and looked into the smiling face of Chris.

'What took you so long?' I said, greatly relieved that he was still there. I was holding my throbbing face and trying to grin. Still clutched tightly in my hand was the diary.

'Sorry mate, had to make some arrangements,' he said with a wink, then added, 'move it! Let's get the fuck out of here and take that scum from the Merc with us.' We lifted the bloke out through the windscreen and threw him in the back of the lorry. We then quickly checked the Merc over – no Si.

The lorry pulled away and all of Chris's blokes disappeared as quickly as they had arrived, leaving some very beat-up bodies on the grass. Chris told Wivva and the others where to meet us and they ran off to get the van; he then climbed into the Toyota with Mick, Tony and me and we moved off after the truck. I sat very quietly in the back while Chris told Mick where to go.

This can't be happening, I thought. Stuff like this only happens in the movies. I tried to put it all in some sort of order. My face hurt like hell and I could feel the blood running down my neck and into my T-shirt.

I must have dozed off, because the next thing that I remember was waking up in what looked like a lorry park. Unhitched trailers were everywhere. Behind me was Mick's van, it was empty. Next to me was the lorry that had wiped out the Merc. I got out, walked over and checked the cab. No one home. I caught a glance at myself in the side mirror, I nearly shit a brick. The whole of the left side of my face was a bright red and running along my jaw line was a long cut covered with thick dried blood. Trails of blood had run down my neck, under the collar of my leather jacket and soaked the left shoulder of my T-shirt. I was really pissed off to see a long jagged tear running down the right arm of my new leather jacket.

I heard a noise from the back of the lorry so I walked around and pulled the door open. Everyone was inside.

'Oh, sleeping beauty's awake,' said Mick. 'How're you feeling?'

'Bit of an 'eadache,' I said. 'But other than that okay. How long was I out?'

'Only about an hour,' he said. 'You looked so peaceful we thought we'd leave you. Climb up and join the fun.'

I climbed in and looked at everyone. I'd never seen so many bumps, bruises and cuts all in one place at the same time.

'Good job you got there,' Wivva was saying to Chris. 'Otherwise I would have killed them.'

Mick laughed and brought me up to date.

'Chris called one of his friends from my place last night and set it up for some people to help us out. Thank fuck he did, because those scumbags had us well and truly beaten.'

'So even this lorry belongs to Chris?' I said.

'It's my cousin's,' said Chris. 'The back's handy, we can keep the shitbag here for months if we want to. It's insulated. It's a freezer truck so no sounds, and if this turd gets stroppy,' he said, nodding towards the bloke that we had picked up, 'then we just switch on the motor, shut the doors and freeze his fucking bollocks off.'

'Now we wait for the creep to wake up so we ask him about Si,' said Mick. 'We'll also find out if he's the one who's gonna talk to the Old Bill. That bit might take a bit of persuading though,' he said with a wink.

'Alan should have been here for this,' I said. 'He'd have had this shit talking in no time.'

'Leave it to me,' said Wivva as he pulled out the shotgun and started spinning it like he was John Wayne or something.

'I hope that ain't loaded,' said Chris.

'Course it ai . . .' Wivva didn't finish because the gun went off, the pellets whizzing past our ears and out of the open doors. We threw ourselves to the floor, covering our heads with our arms.

The smoke cleared and we saw Wivva standing there with his eyes clamped tightly shut, holding on to the gun and shaking from head to foot. Chris jumped up and grabbed the gun.

'I think I'd better take that back now,' he said with a grin. We were all more than just a little relieved.

After a bit of 'friendly persuasion' the bloke gave us all

that we needed on Si. He was supposed to ring Gus on his bleeper number when he'd got the diary and leave a message for him to ring home. He was then to take the book over to the Highbury house and wait for Gus to arrive later with Si.

'The boy wasn't going to be hurt until the diary was safe in Gus's hands,' said the guy and added, 'for insurance.' If all went well, Gus would aim to get to his house by about four that afternoon.

'What if one of those that we left behind warns him?' I asked.

Chris laughed and said, 'Don't worry, they won't be in any mood to talk to anyone for at least twenty-four hours.' He then wrote down the number that the bloke had to ring and said, 'Let's go to Highbury, lads.'

We tied the bloke up in a sack, took his keys and left him in the corner. We then jumped out, slammed and locked the doors and drove off, switching on the lorry's freezer motor first.

Chapter Twenty-one

It was still early. The only people about seemed to be the milkman and the paper boy, so we parked up around the corner and entered the house silently in twos. It was empty, so we decided to make ourselves at home.

Chris rang the bleeper number and left the message. I was lumbered with the job of preparing breakfast.

'Well, you are a chef,' said Mick.

The rest started to check out the house. Wivva found a wall safe in the front room and started to fuck about with the combination. Pete and Den found the sound system and tuned into Capital Gold, then they busied themselves with opening drawers and cupboards, checking out the contents. Chris and Mick found his office. There was so much there that Chris convinced Mick to leave it until after they had eaten. Tony took a shower. Tony always took showers, sometimes three or even four a day; it was a part of his problem and his way of dealing with his feelings of being dirty all the time.

After we had eaten, eggs, bacon, sausages, beans, fried bread, cake, biscuits, orange juice, coffee, tea, all of his fruit and anything else that we could find, we all decided to follow Tony's example and clean ourselves up. Thank fuck he had a big bathroom and plenty of towels, his washing bill after we had finished was gonna cost him an arm and a leg.

I was very relieved to find that the cut on my face wasn't as bad as I had thought; in fact it was more of a scratch than a cut. Just like when you cut yourself shaving, loads of blood, but you're hard pressed to see where it's coming from. A wipe over, dab of disinfectant, and a plaster on the worst bit and I was fine.

Wivva went back to the safe while the rest of us went through the house bit by bit, leaving his office till last.

The radio was blaring out 'You Ain't Seen Nothing Yet' when we opened the door to his bedroom at the top of the house. Boy was that song right. It was by far the worst room in the house. We stood gobsmacked at what we saw. The ceiling was covered with mirrors, porno books and videos were everywhere. There was also a whole selection of sex aids, handcuffs, chains, even a couple of blow-up blondes were sitting in the corner, legs splayed, mouths agape. The whole room had also been sound-proofed. We didn't need much of an imagination to figure out why.

'Guess he must entertain a lot,' said Mick, trying to lighten the mood a bit.

'Filthy bastard!' said Chris. 'What makes people like this?'

On the table by the bed was a small brass chest, and inside was at least half a kilo of cocaine, plus spoons, tubes and cutters.

'That's a nice bit of snow,' said Mick and he took a snort from between pinched fingers, then rubbed his fingertips on his gums. He smiled, so we all, except for

Chris, followed suit.

Big mistake.

Heads started to go fuzzy, brains began to lose control. Mick clicked on a combined telly and video and we saw a few seconds of a child porn film before we shut it down. The videos were stacked in order on shelves, each of them bearing the names of the people in them written on the box. I looked through them and found one with the MP's name on it.

'Why should he have the names on these?' I asked nobody in particular.

'Who knows why this shit does anything,' offered Mick.

'Could be blackmail meat,' suggested Chris. 'Look at those names, he's got each of them exactly where he wants them. I doubt if any of them even knew that they were being filmed. These look like master copies, for his use only. I'll bet he even uses them to impress his guests.'

Mick ripped off a padlock, opened a cupboard and whistled. Chris and me moved over to take a look. It was full of devil worship stuff, books on bestiality, paedophile contact magazines and very hard-core child porn.

'Caters for every need doesn't he?' said Mick, staring at the stuff. Chris picked up a pile of photos and flicked through them. He gagged and throwing them to the back of the cupboard pushed past us and rushed into the en suite bathroom. He vomited and heaved for at least five minutes before he came up for air.

'For fuck's sake,' he said, still choking, 'how can people do those sorts of things to kids? They've got to be evil, really fucking evil.'

Tony called us back to the bedroom.

'Look at this,' he said and switched the TV on again.

'We've seen it,' I said.

'Not this you haven't,' he said. 'I found it under the shelf with three others. They're snuff movies.'

'You what?' said Chris. He was still feeling more than a little fragile and I don't think he really wanted to know.

'Snuff movies,' repeated Tony. 'Y'know, it's when they kill someone for real and film it.'

'Oh, for God's sake!' moaned Chris. 'Doesn't it ever fucking end?'

We left the room, we couldn't wait for Gus to get home.

Wivva was still working on the safe. Come to think of it, he'd been working on that safe, on and off, ever since we'd got there and he was now getting the 'right hump' with it.

Chris took a look and said, 'No chance, you won't get into that through the front.'

He then went through the kitchen and into the garage to see if he could find something that could help. He came back with a club hammer, a crowbar and a few cold chisels. I think that he was happy to have found something to do that would keep his mind off the shit that he had seen upstairs. Anyway, keeping the noise down as much as possible and using the club hammer and crowbar, he ripped the safe clean out of the wall. He laid it on its face and started to cut away at the back with the hammer and cold chisel. It took over an hour before he could bend the panel down enough to take out what was inside. We could see that he'd done it before, he was very efficient.

While we watched, Pete and Den must have pushed

something on the bookcase at the back of the room, because a whole section swung open revealing a fully stocked bar. The slag even had lager on draught. Needless to say, we made full use of it.

The safe was now empty and on the floor in front of it were piles of fifty-pound notes still in their bank wrappers.

'Loadsamoney!' Wivva shouted and started to count it.

There was another small book full of names. I flicked through it and recognised a few of them. I couldn't believe two of them, I'd watched and heard these people on radio and telly for years. I showed the others. They all agreed that the sooner the Old Bill started looking at this lot the better. Mick got his Rolex. It was exactly the same as mine.

'Must have got a job lot,' I said.

We made eight thousand, four hundred pounds each. Wivva had laid it out in nine neat piles.

'There's one too many,' said Chris.

'No, you get a share,' said Mick.

'Thanks, but there's still one too many,' he said again.

'Eight grand should buy a brilliant funeral and headstone for Alan,' said Mick.

Chris nodded, smiled and said, 'Nice one.'

We all sat down and started to discuss for the first time what it was that we were going to do. Until then I thought that we were going to get Si back, give Gus a good spanking and then piss off and leave him to the police. Chris said that we needed more than that. He said that if Gus was in with the locals and they were called in, then anything could happen, and if it wasn't the locals, then it seemed fair to expect him to have one or two very high contacts within the police, who could influence any investigation.

'We've got to let your brief's copper know then,' said Mick.

'We've got to get Si back first,' I said, 'and then we decide what to do.'

'Sounds good to me,' said Chris. 'We'll play it by ear until we know that Si's safe. But whatever we do, we make sure that he goes down for a very long time, even if it means calling the papers before we call the Bill.'

Everyone agreed.

I switched on the telly. *Neighbours* again. It seems that Harold has just been made an earl or a lord or something. I like Harold, he's good. I've often thought that he'd make a brilliant Oliver Hardy.

The afternoon was spent going through the office. It was full of equipment – typewriter, computer, fax, that sort of stuff. In the corner was a photocopier. 'Great,' said Chris and began making copies of the diary and address book. 'Insurance,' he said.

It seemed that the cash in the safe was for an investment. Gus was going to buy his way into a string of sex shops. He also had ledgers and books that showed that he was into loads of other things like car sales, escort services, mini cabs, betting shops, even a sweet shop and tobacconist in Peckham. He also fully owned Fotojoy UK. We learned a lot about the guy that day and with each new piece of information, we hated him more.

At half-past three I was looking through the blinds keeping an eye out for Gus. Up the road, still wrapped around a tree, was the burned out Granada that Alan had totalled. Tapes and barriers had been put around it by the police. A copper was standing beside it with his arms behind his back; he looked thoroughly pissed off. Also taped off was the place where Alan was found. We'd all drunk, snorted and smoked far too much.

A Ford Sierra cruised softly down the road from the top end and turned quietly into the drive. I motioned to the guys to be quiet. I could see two figures in the car. It stopped and the driver got out; it was Gus, it couldn't be anyone else. He walked up the road to where the copper was, stopped and started to talk to him.

'What the fuck's he up to?' Mick whispered in my ear.

The passenger door opened and the other guy got out, he opened the back door and dragged little Si out from under a blanket and took him into the garage. That's why Gus was talking to the copper, I thought, to keep his attention away from the house. Mick and Chris went into the kitchen and waited by the connecting door to the garage.

We heard the key turn in the lock and just as the door was about to be pushed open, Mick grabbed it and pulled hard. The guy came flying into the room head first and landed in a heap by the sink. Wivva hit him with the hammer knocking him spark out. Poor old Si just stood there crying buckets.

'He must be happy to see us,' said Mick. Then he took him to one side while we waited for Gus.

'Point to which door,' said Chris. I nodded and watched. Gus left the copper and walked back to the house. He calmly locked his motor, pushed the garage doors shut and walked up to the front door.

'Front door,' I hissed. Chris slipped behind it and Mick slid into an alcove on the other side.

The door opened, Gus walked in and pushed it shut behind him. He was folding his keys back up into their leather case when Mick said, 'Hi, Gus.' Gus turned and was about to shout when Chris whacked him full in the throat. He collapsed choking for air.

When he looked up we were all standing around him in a circle.

'Hi, Gus,' we said together, 'nice to meet you.'

Si had been handcuffed and had tape across his mouth. Chris gently removed it and with the key that he'd ripped from the chain on Gus's trousers, he undid the cuffs and started rubbing Si's wrists to get the circulation going.

'Did he hurt you son?' he asked.

'They slapped me around me a bit when they snatched me, but they've not touched me since. I'm starving hungry though, any nosh about?'

'You're all right,' said Chris with a laugh and tossed him an apple. 'I'll see what's left in the fridge.'

'Anything you want boys, anything, it's yours,' said Gus. He was still on the floor recovering from the smack in the throat.

'There's nothing you've got that we want,' I said.

'Money,' he said. 'There's money.'

'No, there ain't,' said Mick.

'There is,' he said. 'It's in the safe.'

'No there ain't,' said Wivva.

'There is, I tell you, there is.' He was looking worried.

'There ain't,' I said again. 'We took it ages ago. There's nothing in the safe now.' He began to panic.

'I can get you more,' he said.

'Can you?' asked Chris. 'How much?'

'We don't want his money,' I said, scowling at Chris.

'I was only asking, Stu. You can't blame a bloke for asking, can you?' he said.

'Knock it on the head you two,' said Mick, sensing that I was getting angry at Chris. He then turned to Gus and said, 'We don't want your stinking money. There's nothing you've got that we do want. Nothing at all.'

'Drugs then,' he said. 'Come on boys, you know how hard it is to get anything decent these days. Anything you want, I've got it.'

'Already got them,' said Wivva, going cross-eyed from the joint that he was puffing on. Underneath his arm was the brass chest. Gus saw it and swallowed hard. He had nothing else to offer.

'What do you want then?' he said. He was shaking from head to foot now.

'You,' said Wivva.

'You,' said Mick. Then one after another the rest of us said 'You'. He started to cry, Chris hit him again and he shut up.

We were going to get him to write a full confession, but his hands were shaking so much that he couldn't hold a pen. We tried to get him to talk into a tape-recorder but all he did was blubber and wail. He was making us all fucking angry. This big, powerful man was no more than a snivelling coward when it came to the crunch.

We dragged him and his pal up the stairs to his bedroom. We thought that if we took him there, we could somehow make him produce evidence that we needed to put him and his cronies away. We weren't thinking straight, the booze and drugs were making us lose control.

We all had ideas about what we wanted to do but no two ideas were the same. And none of us, by that time, was in any condition to discuss the matter.

Mick and me wrapped a carpet around Gus's pal and dumped him in the corner with the two blow-ups. Chris and Wivva were holding Gus down on his bed.

Everything seemed to be happening in slow motion, so we all took another snort of coke, thinking that it would wake us up. It didn't. Cannabis, coke and alcohol just don't mix. We walked around like zombies, everything was going on automatic. We all had just one thought, and that thought was Gus and what we could do to him.

'Kill him,' said Wivva, raising his hammer. 'Smash his fucking head in.'

'No hurt him, really hurt him,' said Tony.

'Easy lads,' said Chris. 'We've got to get from him what we want first. We don't want to fuck this up.'

'No Chris,' I said. 'What you want.'

'Come on, Stu,' said Chris. 'I want this guy to go away as much as any of you, but we've got to do it properly. After what he's done to Si, and what we've seen in this stinking house, we can't afford to fuck it up.'

'Bollocks to all that. Kill him,' Wivva slurred. 'He killed Alan.'

'That was nothing to do with me,' Gus wailed. 'It was that stupid bastard in the corner.' Wivva turned and walked towards the guy wrapped in the carpet, his hammer at the ready. Chris jumped over and grabbed his wrist. 'Hang on Wivva,' he said. 'You don't need that. Look at him.' We all looked at the guy. His head had fallen back, his eyes were wide open and rolled up, his mouth gaped, a bubbly foam running from the corner.

'He's gone,' said Chris. 'His heart's given out.'

'Lucky bastard,' said Wivva and he turned back to Gus. Gus shat himself.

'Keep him off me! Keep him off me!' he screamed. He then jumped from the bed shrugging Tony aside as he made a bolt for the door. Wivva threw the hammer at his head, he ducked and the hammer thudded into the wall lodging there. We all stood rooted to the spot and watched as Gus lost his footing and rolled out of the door, smashed through the banister rail and fell screaming down the stairwell. Three floors he fell, head first on to quarry tiles. We rushed down to check him, it wasn't a pretty sight. Still I guess it solved our problem.

We had to leave, but this time we weren't laughing. This time we were all deadly serious. This time we had gone much too far. No one spoke, we just cleaned ourselves up, wiped everything that we had touched and left, taking care not to let the copper up the road see us.

Mick took Gus's pen and the Sierra. I've not touched a joint or had a snort since. Those fucking drugs robbed us of the chance of seeing that shit go down for a very long time, and possibly the chance of taking all of his perverted friends with him.

Chapter Twenty-two

For two days we sat at Mick's, barely saying a word to each other. Chris said that he would hang on for a couple of days before he gave all the information to his brief, so we were waiting to see what would happen.

I went to Greenford, but couldn't stay long, I wasn't very good company. Beryl sussed that something very serious was wrong with me, but didn't push it. I needed time on my own, time to think, time to take in what I had done. I told Mick.

'Thank fuck for that,' he said. 'I thought I was the only one.' We all decided to split up for a few days.

Just before my mum left, she took Jen, Ali and me to Jaywick for a week on holiday. We stayed in a chalet by the seafront. I remembered coming out of the chalet very early every morning and going straight on to the beach. I loved it, especially when the sea was a bit rough. The spray used to fly through the air as the waves hit the breakers, its smell and feel seemed like magic to me. When I said this to Mick he said, 'No problem. There's a motor downstairs, why not use it.'

The drive was much quicker than I had remembered. I

seemed to be there in no time. I drove straight to the seafront.

It wasn't how I remembered it, but then nothing really is.

I parked up the Sierra and walked along the front. It was getting dark.

On my right were the chalets, all lit up. Rows and rows of them.

I found the one that I thought I had stayed in all those years ago. I was sure it was, though it was now a different colour. This one was a kind of yellow and red and ours had been blue, but I was sure that this was it. There was a way of checking, I remembered. When I was a kid, I was always getting a clout around the head for fucking around with my penknife. I used to carve my name into everything. Mum kicked my arse for doing it at the chalet. Right on top of the handrail on the balcony at the front it was.

I crossed over the road and climbed the few steps up on to the front of the chalet and began to check the handrail. There it was. It was covered with God knows how many layers of paint, but there it was – 'S S 19 . . .'. I was going to carve 1978 but Mum caught me before I could finish it.

The door swung open and an old dear stood there.

''Ere, what's your game,' she said.

'Sorry, love,' I said. 'Wrong place, wrong time.' I walked down the steps and away. I heard her call to her old man, 'Louieee! You make sure that you lock up properly tonight, there's some funny people about.'

I got back to the car and sat there for a while. No, it wasn't really the same at all.

I drove up through Clacton and on to Walton. I found a quiet place that overlooked the sea, parked up and sat staring out at it. I fell asleep.

When I awoke, it was early morning. I looked at my watch, it was almost five. I got out of the car, stretched and decided to walk to the beach. There were two joggers running over the sands, so I sat down to watch them.

They had obviously been running for some time because their tracksuits were drenched with sweat. The girl turned and ran towards the water, the bloke chased her. They fell over each other into the sea, the girl was squealing and laughing with delight. I felt dead jealous, my eyes began to sting.

'Fucking sea air,' I said to myself as I took out a hanky and blew my nose. It didn't work. I sat there and cried like a baby. Best cry I've ever had that was.

I was starving, so I got up and walked towards the shops on the front. I found the public lavatories, went in and swilled my face. I felt a lot better. I then had a giant breakfast in a transport café just off the front, walked back to the car and drove back to London.

I woke Mick up with a big mug of tea.

'Can't stay away eh?' he said bleary-eyed as I went back to the kitchen. I came back with a tray on which was a full English breakfast.

'Fucking hell,' he said. 'Breakfast in bed too. What have I done to deserve all this?'

Now Mick is one of those blokes who can't face anything in the morning until he's had at least three cups of tea and three smokes, his stomach just won't take it. But he sat there and ate everything that I had prepared for him, and what's more, he even said that it was great. I really appreciated him for that.

We decided to start sorting out everything that day, while we had the time to ourselves. Si was with his uncle Chris, Pete, Den and Wivva had gone home for a while and Tony had gone to stay with his nan for a few days.

We visited Ali first, taking her a massive bowl of fruit and some flowers.

'Oh, Stu,' she said. 'Where have you been, we've all been so worried?'

'Sorry, toots,' I said. 'I had some things to do.'

'Like what?' she asked.

'None of your business,' I replied. 'Let's just say that you don't ever have to worry again about the old man or Gus and his goons.'

'Why? What have you done?' she asked.

'Nothing, honest. They just went a bit overboard.' Mick coughed and looked at the ceiling.

'And as a result,' I continued. 'They've gone away for ever.'

'Police?' she asked.

'Something like that,' I said.

'Are you sure about this Stu?' She looked very serious.

'Would I lie?' I said, palms upwards and shrugging my shoulders.

'Guess what, Stu? I can leave tomorrow,' she said.

'Brilliant!' I yelled. 'I'll zoom over to Beryl's now and make all the arrangements.'

'What about the house?' she asked.

'Let the council have it back,' I said. 'Too many bad memories.'

'It's not the council's any more,' she said. 'He bought it

from them, cash. Two years ago.'

'Even better,' I said. 'Then we can flog it and get something else. Look, don't worry about it now, let me get over to Beryl's and make the arrangements to get you out of here first.'

'Okay, love,' she said.

'First thing tomorrow,' I said. 'We'll be back first thing tomorrow.' We said goodbye and left.

I phoned Beryl, gave her the good news about Ali and said that I would pop over later to see them. She told me to bring Mick with me for dinner. We then drove down to see Chris.

'The Bill have raided the house and cleaned it out,' he said. 'My brief assures me that they are looking for nobody in connection with any deaths and that I pass on the grateful thanks of his friend for a job well done. The bloke in the freezer was picked up and is singing like a bird. It seems that he was very near to freezing to death. Thankfully the unit was on at a low setting. Anyway, he's been arrested in connection with allegations of sexual abuse of children, and more arrests are expected. The copper dealing with it will be on the news tonight.

'My brief suggested that I send copies of the diary and address book to a bloke on one of the papers that has been exposing this sort of thing. I took them to him today, he even bought Si and me lunch. He said that it was the best evidence that he had ever seen to prove that some very influential people are running or are involved in the sexual abuse of children. He will be working closely with my brief to watch and make sure that all that needs to be said publicly, will be, and then he will expose the whole bloody lot in his newspaper. He also said that he would like at some time to talk to all of you. I told him that I would ask, but that he wasn't to hold out any hopes.

'It's over, Stu, Mick. You can get on with your lives again. You can relax now. By the way,' he said finally, 'the social services say that I can keep Si. My brief arranged it through a friend of his.'

'That's brilliant,' I said.

'Magic,' Mick said.

'Where is he then?' I asked.

'Who?' said Chris.

'Si, you berk,' I said.

'Ah, well I thought you would ask that,' he said. 'I'm afraid that we've got some problems with Si at the moment. I didn't want to tell you, as, well, quite frankly, you've got more than enough problems of your own to worry about at the moment.'

'What's wrong, Chris?' I asked.

'To tell you the truth, I think he's shit scared,' said Chris. 'After the Gus thing, he couldn't sleep, he'd just lay there in a cold sweat. We got very worried. I couldn't call in the doctor in case Si said something that he shouldn't. He shouldn't have been at that house you know. He shouldn't have seen all that shit. It's affected him quite badly. I blame myself, I should have known better.'

'No, it's my fault,' I said. 'I knew he was just a kid.'

'What a load of bollocks,' said Mick. 'You both know damn well that neither of you could have stopped him, and sitting here talking about who's to blame ain't gonna help the poor fucker either. Where is he, Chris?'

'In the back,' he said. Chris took us through to the back room.

Si was sitting cross-legged in a big fluffy armchair by

the french windows, a steaming mug of tea in his hands. He was staring through the window and off up into space. He seemed miles away.

He couldn't have heard us come in because when Mick said, 'Hello, mate' and touched his shoulder, he jumped, spilling some of his tea on to his legs.

'Fucking Jesus!' he yelped as he dropped his mug on the floor and jumped to his feet, pulling the fabric of his tracksuit bottoms away from the skin of his legs. 'Ow! Ow! Shit! That hurts. What the fucking hell you doing creeping up on someone like that?'

Me and Mick were laughing as Si hopped first on one leg then the other, and pulling the legs of his tracksuit up to check his shins.

'Oi! That's a new bloody carpet,' yelled Chris as he rushed over. He pushed Si aside and threw down a newspaper to soak up the spilled tea. 'The wife'll kill me,' he said as he stamped on the paper. Si landed back in his chair with his legs kicking the air. He looked really daft. That set me and Mick off into hysterics even more.

'It ain't funny,' Si yelled at us, trying hard not to laugh, but he couldn't do it. His face cracked and he doubled up.

Chris looked at him, shook his head and said, 'And here's me thinking you were depressed.'

That only set us off again, even Chris joined in. It was funny, but I was more pleased that Si looked his old self again.

Chapter Twenty-three

'Police raided a house in Highbury in the early hours of this morning, after a tip off,' said the guy on the news, 'and discovered the bodies of two men. It is thought that there is some connection between this and the deaths of three men in an incident in the street earlier this week. We pass you now to our reporter on the scene.'

The picture changed to a man standing by a pair of garage doors.

'The house is still a hive of activity,' he said. 'Police have removed at least two vanloads of material indicating that the owner of this house was involved in paedophilia and the selling of child pornography. I have beside me the senior officer in charge of this investigation.' He moved over and shoved his microphone in the face of a guy standing by the front steps. 'Can you tell me, Superintendent,' he said, 'just what it is that you've found here today?'

'We've discovered at this house what could be some of the most significant information that we have ever had, concerning organised child sexual abuse in this country,' said the copper. 'There are books full of names and addresses of people who could be involved, plus a mass of information about the various rings and cells that seem to exist in London and the Home Counties. We are very, very excited with this find, although of course sad that our worst fears are being realised.'

'Is it true then,' said the reporter, 'that the names of some very well-known people have been found on those lists?'

'I cannot comment on that at this time,' said the policeman, 'but I do promise that if any of the names listed are proved to be involved in any way, then whoever they are, they shall feel the full weight of the law.'

'And the deaths?' said the reporter. 'Five men died here this week. Are they all connected with this matter?'

'Yes, indeed. I fully believe that there was some sort of internal struggle within this particular gang, and that developed into open warfare.'

'At least while they are killing each other off, they are saving you the trouble of catching them,' said the reporter.

'Precisely,' said the superintendent with a grin.

'Thank you,' said the reporter, 'and now back to the studio.'

Jen and Beryl turned to look at Mick and me. Jen's face was an absolute picture.

'That was Gus's house,' she said, her eyes wide.

'Hmm, hmm,' I mumbled, looking at Mick and smiling.

'Was he one of those . . .?'

'Hmm, hmm,' Mick mumbled, smiling back.

'Serves him right,' she said. 'I knew they'd kill each other one day.'

'Hmm, hmm,' mumbled Mick and me together now grinning.

Bless her, I thought. Oh to be so innocent.

Beryl said nothing.

We made a lot of arrangements that night, Beryl making one that blew us apart and also solved most of our problems.

With the sale of the house at Crouch End and the sale of her bungalow, she suggested that we buy a large place, big enough for Ali, Jen, Cheri, me and her to live together as a family.

'As you know,' she said, 'Chef and me were never blessed with children and it's something that I've always regretted. I'd like to do this, if only for the girls.'

'Please say yes,' said Jen. 'Please.'

'Sounds good to me,' I said and Jen rushed over and threw her arms around my neck. Mick and me then helped get the front room ready for the arrival of the invalid.

Mick came with me to collect Ali. When we got there she was ready and waiting for us. Both of her arms were still in plaster casts and were held close to her chest in slings. The drips and tubes had all been removed and she was complaining that for the first time since she had come into hospital, she was bursting for a pee. The nurse took her to the toilet while the ward sister gave us all the medication she needed and the written instructions for her care at home. She also gave us a letter for her doctor.

The nurse brought Ali back to say goodbye to the other patients and the ward sister, then we went down to the car. Me pushing the wheelchair and Mick and the nurse carrying her stuff.

The drive to Greenford wasn't without incident. We had to stop at least five times to let her relax herself.

Every time that we went over a bump it hurt her and she tensed up. She became so tense that she started to get cramps, so we had to stop and let her stretch every so often. She also decided that she fancied an ice-cream, then she wanted a chocolate bar, then a Coke. In fact, we were bloody glad when we arrived at Beryl's.

Jenny and Beryl were clucking around her like old mother hens. Cheri went absolutely crackers when she saw her mum. Everyone was crying again.

Chapter Twenty-four

It'd been almost two months and we still hadn't seen Wivva. Most of that time had been taken up with sorting ourselves out.

Beryl had been making all of the arrangements for the new family home. Ali was much better, Cheri was in play school and coming on in leaps and bounds. Me and the lads met up a few times, not for business or anything, just to hang around and have a bit of fun.

We were all worried about Wivva and hoped that he'd got the message about Alan's funeral. It had taken so long to get permission to bury him because the police had kept him on ice while they finished their investigations. But at last it was time to put him to rest.

Eight thousand, four hundred pounds buys the most amazing funeral.

The coffin shone, real gold handles, pure silk inside. Alan was dressed in a new suit, Georgio Armani. Gucci shoes and a Dior shirt completed the look. His Raybans were placed over his eyes, he loved his shades. He looked the best we'd ever seen him. The undertaker must have worked miracles with his face, not a mark, not a scratch was to be seen.

With the six of us were Beryl with Jen, Ali and Cheri
and Chris and his family. About twenty of our own
friends, past and present had also turned up. Not one of
the slags from Alan's family was to be seen. Not even his
Nan, the one who couldn't cope without him. They never
even sent a card.

We had nine limos with the hearse and a stunning
amount of flowers. The first five motors were full of them.
We had a special done by the florist which was in the
shape of a star with Alan's name across the middle. It
stood four and a half feet high and was mounted on top
of the hearse at the front. The police superintendent sent
some flowers too, that was nice, considering he didn't
even know Alan.

We were just about to move off when we heard a shout
from the top of the road.

'Oi!' it screamed, 'wait for me!' It was Wivva and he
was in a fucking army uniform. He ran, clumping down
the road in his heavy boots. We couldn't believe it.

'What the bloody hell have you done now?' said Mick.

'Joined up, ain't I?' said Wivva. 'I said I would.'

'So that's where you've been all this time then,' said Si.

'Yep, basic training in Colchester.'

'Why didn't you tell us?' asked Mick.

'Are you kidding, you would only have talked me out
of it.'

'You're enjoying it then?' I said.

'Fucking right,' said Wivva. 'Best thing I've ever done.'

'Look out, Iraq, here comes Wivva,' we all said
together.

'Too right,' said Wivva pumping out his chest. 'Too
fucking right.'

We cruised slowly from the funeral parlour in Holloway out to the cemetery in Barnet. All of the motors including the hearse were blasting out Alan's favourite sounds.

You know we all used to take the piss something rotten out of Alan for the stuff he used to listen to, but I don't think anyone could have chosen better for the occasion. For the trip to the cemetery, the Smiths belted out their best. During and after the service, it was Ian Dury and Steve Harley. Alan was well into the Smiths because he was convinced that Morrissey was deaf and he admired Ian Dury because he was handicapped. He thought it was fucking brilliant how they had overcome their problems and made it big.

As for Steve Harley? Well it was just the name of his band, Cockney Rebel. Alan lived that name to the full.

We all carried his coffin into the chapel. The service was a bit heavy, we all cried, but Alan would have agreed that we did him proud. The headstone had his name and the dates of his birth and death, and in big gold letters, on the black marble were the words:

THE
MAGNIFICENT
ONE

We all went back to Max's, he amazed us with a five-course meal and all the booze that we could handle. We had to pay him mind you, in advance.

We were about to tuck into the meal when Max stood on a chair and called for all of us to be quiet. He looked at us and said, 'I would like you all to raise your glasses please, to toast the memory of a boy who tragically had his life taken from him, when he had so much left to live for. A toast please to Alan, a very nice young man, a young man who knew the true meaning of friendship.'

Max looked at us all when he spoke those last words. We knew exactly what he meant. We all toasted Alan.

I started to fill up again. With all that was going on, none of us had remembered to toast Alan's memory. I was full of admiration for Max for doing that for us.

Alan, if you're listening, mate, we miss you.

Chapter Twenty-five
Epilogue

Alan's funeral seemed to change us all. It's hard to explain but it was like we all no longer had a need to be together. The job was done and we were free at last to get on with our lives. We'd had enough of all of the violence and hurt. Enough of the sleaze and corruption and disgusting old men with their disgusting needs. It was time for us all to change, time to find another way of living. All of us that is except Mick.

Mick was obsessed with getting the MP. Long after we had all gone our different ways Mick would still haunt the addresses in the book, in the hope that he could catch the MP at it. It took him six months or so before he had any success.

He arrived at an address in South London late one night and saw the MP's Roller parked outside. Unable to do anything about the activities that he was sure were going on inside the house, he set fire to the car, nicked its Silver Lady emblem and legged it just before it blew up scattering burning debris all over the place. He took the emblem to Alan's grave and fixed it to the headstone. That was joined shortly after by a Jaguar emblem from the car of one of the television personalities whose name was in the book.

When Mick's not working he can almost always be found at Alan's graveside, where he just sits and talks. There's no happy ending for Mick, though he'd never admit that. I make sure that I see him whenever I can.

Wivva was the first to show us that there is a life other than the life that we had been living. By joining the army he'd made a whole new life for himself.

He made it to Iraq, they even gave him his own gun, silly bastards. His first letter to us from there told us in great detail what had happened to a rat that had been foolish enough to run across his gun sight when he was on the practice range.

'Five rounds rapid fire,' he wrote, 'and the rat was history. No arse, no head, no nothing.'

A short time later he was nicked by the Military Police for going AWOL with a French Foreign Legion soldier named Albert who comes, believe it or not, from Hebden Bridge up in Yorkshire or something. It seems that they had nicked a load of booze from the American camp and got caught trying to sell it to their mates. So they did a runner. Wivva reckoned that he was lucky to be in the British Army because his mate got two years hard from the French. He only got one month and a caution. He's due back in a couple of weeks, so we are all going to get together, go out and get totally rat-arsed.

Si's settled down really nicely with Uncle Chris and family. He's back in school and actually seems to like it. He's going for his GCSEs soon. The streets are something that Si used to do now, there's no need any more.

I think the best thing is that Si has at last stopped sniffing. Chris took him up to the hospital and they found that he had a simple sinus problem. A small operation later and he was totally cured. No more sniffing, no more runny nose. Chris is really pissed off that no one cared enough about the kid to go and get him checked out sooner, especially when you see the change in him since that operation. He's like a whole new kid. He's happier and more confident now than he's ever been.

Pete and Den got the idea into their heads that they could start a rock group. Trouble is that no one told them that they would actually have to be able to play their instruments, and strumming blow-up guitars at Quo concerts wasn't really the best way to learn. It was a disaster of course, but they had a lot of fun trying. They are now working for a bloke who touts tickets around the West End and can be seen most weekends working the queues outside the theatres. They seem happy enough.

Tony's back with his mum. Lovely story this. He went to visit her, he says, to get her out of his system. But when she opened the door, she flung her arms around him, hugged him tight and cried her bleeding eyes out. He started blubbing too. She dragged him inside and they sat and talked for hours. The result is that she wants him to live with her again and rebuild their lives together. You know, all Tony ever wanted was his mother's love and now he's got it, we're all really chuffed for him.

Beryl and the girls sold up and bought a big house out in the sticks. Ali's working and Jen is looking for work. Cheri is brilliant, she's in school and is getting on really well. If you didn't know better, you would swear that nothing had ever happened to her. Beryl's in her element caring for them all.

As for me, well, I got my job back at the hotel. The new chef didn't want me because I'd let him down by leaving without telling him, but for some reason George pulled some strings with his family and I was taken back. I really feel shitty now about the way I treated him before.

I went back to college, got my qualifications, and I'm soon going to be second chef. Beryl and the girls threw a big party for me when I qualified.

I've also got a steady girlfriend now, we've been going together for some time. So much so that Ali and Jen are on my back trying to get me to make an honest woman of her. No chance. I've seen what marriage can do to people. And as for having kids, well they can forget that, I'm not bringing any kids into this shitty world.

You know, all this time later and still no one's been done for all that shit we uncovered. Even the geezer we shut in the freezer truck was released. All that work for nothing, eh?

Mick'll continue doing his bit I'm sure, and if he ever needs us, we're there for him. But I often wonder why the Old Bill didn't do anything. Was it because they couldn't? Or wouldn't? Were they stopped from acting by the MP and his cronies? Or were some of the Old Bill themselves involved? Maybe I'll never know, but one thing's for sure, I'm never going back to the way that I was, doing the things that I did. Not because I'm ashamed of it or anything, though to be honest, we did do some very stupid things during that time. But because there is no room for that shit in my life any more. After all, I've now got responsibilities, I'm gonna be the best chef this town's ever seen and have a restaurant that's second to none. Maybe I'll even be a telly cook. Well, a man can dream, can't he . . .